MOUNTAIN RISE RANCH

A Montana Country Inn Romance Novel – Book 2

AMY RAFFERTY

STAY UPDATED WITH ME

Thank you so much for purchasing or downloading my book! I am grateful to all my amazing readers.

To stay updated on all my latest books, newsletters, freebies and beautiful photos from the fabulous locations I write about, why not join my VIP group?

I will send you regular pictures of La Jolla Cove, San Diego and the Florida Gulf Beaches where I try to spend as much time as I can. I live in San Diego, my own 'Garden Of Eden' and I am in love with the sea and the beaches in the area. They inspire me to write lots of beachy mystery romance fiction to share with my awesome readers like you. To join me go to https://landing.mailer lite.com/webforms/landing/y6w2d2

You will be asked for your email. You also get a FREE BOOK whenever you sign-up!

FREE BOOK

To get your FREE copy of Cody Bay Inn Prequel - Nantucket Calling go to www.amazon.com/B0992NFTY1

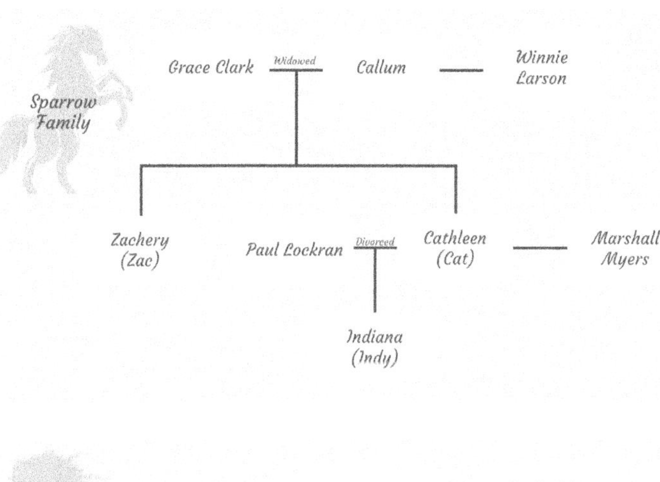

Sparrow Family
Grace Clark
Widowed
Callum
Winnie Larson
Zachery (Zac)
Paul Lockran
Divorced
Cathleen (Cat)
Marshall Myers
Indiana (Indy)

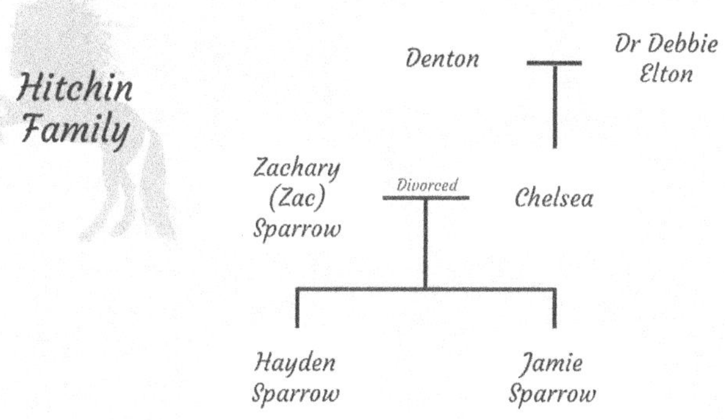

Hitchin Family
Denton
Dr Debbie Elton
Zachary (Zac) Sparrow
Divorced
Chelsea
Hayden Sparrow
Jamie Sparrow

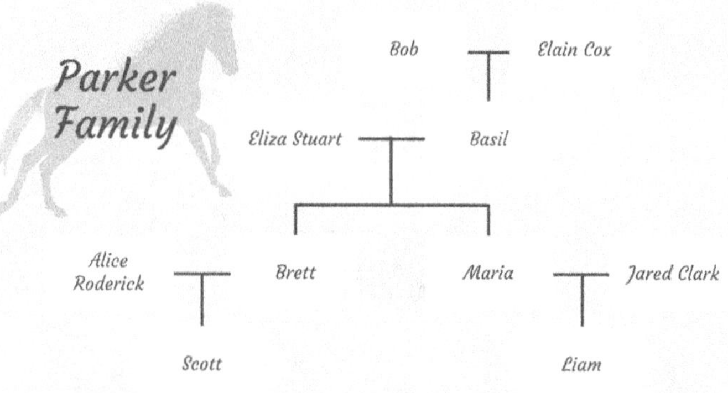

Parker Family
Bob
Elain Cox
Eliza Stuart
Basil
Alice Roderick
Brett
Maria
Jared Clark
Scott
Liam

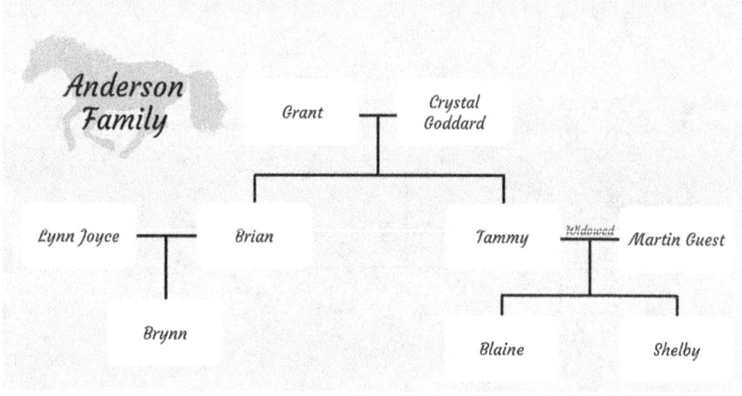

Anderson Family
Grant
Crystal Goddard
Lynn Joyce
Brian
Tammy
Widowed
Martin Guest
Brynn
Blaine
Shelby

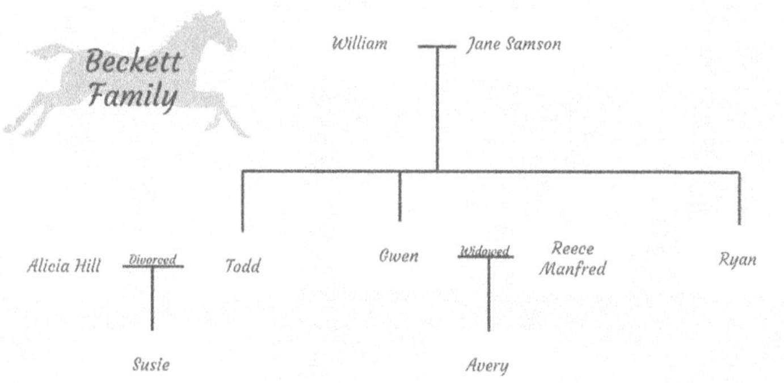

Beckett Family
William
Jane Samson
Alicia Hill
Divorced
Todd
Gwen
Widowed
Reece Manfred
Ryan
Susie
Avery

MAP OF THE RANCHES

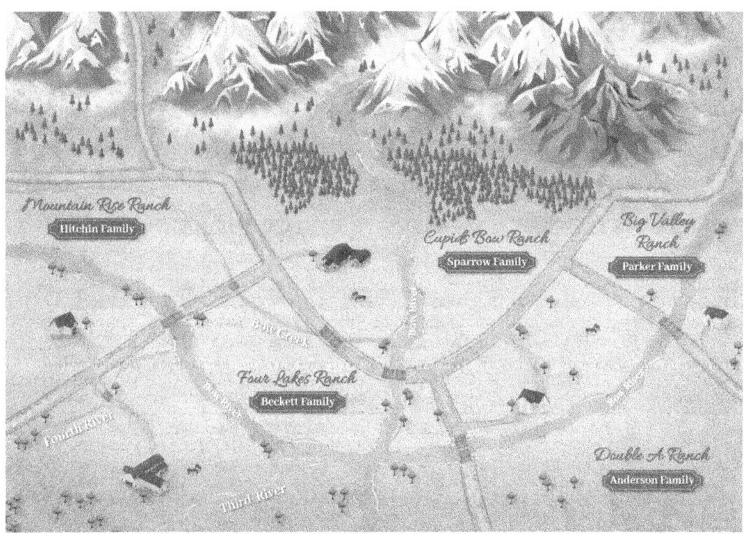

Chapter One

ENDINGS AND RENEWALS

Chelsea Hitchin's face ached from the smile she'd plastered on it the whole day. She felt like a clown with a painted smile and a bright red nose. Chelsea's bright red nose was concealed under layers of makeup, just like her swollen puffy eyes. She couldn't be a good host if she looked like she was a complete wreck. Expect that was exactly what Chelsea felt like at the moment. Thank goodness for her two adult children and her friends, Ashley Cuthbert-Hall, and Cat Sparrow. Even Maria Parker and her brother, Brett, had come to lend a hand this morning. Chelsea didn't know if she'd have coped without all of them helping her get everything ready for the gathering after the funeral.

Chelsea knew her mother wanted to be buried next to her father on the family plot and then have the gathering at Mountain Rise Ranch. Dr. Debbie Hitchin had even planned out the entire spread months before she'd passed away. Chelsea's mother had wanted to be able to make sure she had everything arranged while she still had moments of clarity. The disease that had taken her mother was a cruel one. Her mother had suffered a massive stroke two years ago and then another smaller one eight months ago. It had caused vascular dementia from the damaged blood vessels caused by the strokes. The strokes had also interfered with Debbie's mobility. Chelsea had never been more grateful for her nursing degree than she had been over these past two years. It ensured she could give her mother the best care possible.

It also helped with the costs. Not that Chelsea would've ever skimped on the costs of her mother's care, and she hadn't. But she knew one day she was going to have to go into her mother's study and face the pile of bills lying there like little money hitmen, waiting to target and drain the life from her bank account. Not that there was much of anything in there right now. Chelsea swallowed and deliberately switched her mind off to the bills and her financial difficulties. Today was not the day to be worrying about them. Today was the day she'd dreaded the most since they'd taken her mother away for the last time. Chelsea knew everyone was only paying their respects and showing just how much they cared for her mother, Debbie, but she didn't know how much more she could take. Chelsea was starting to get a headache and she'd had to sneak off to her room twice now just to breathe and try to alleviate the panic attack threatening to overtake her.

"Everyone's about to leave," Cat said, walking up to Chelsea. "Just a few more minutes, and then everyone will be gone."

"I don't want to seem ungrateful," Chelsea said. She was a little concerned that her guests may think she was being rude because she had escaped to the kitchen for a few minutes.

"They understand what you're going through," Cat told her. "You also have enough food to last you a year."

"We put it in the freezer for you," Ashley said, walking into the kitchen mid-conversation.

"Thank you." Chelsea gave them both a weak smile, which was all she had the strength to muster at the moment. "All of you, for helping me through today and this week."

"Of course," Chelsea and Ashley said together.

"Jamie is going to stay with you. Zac is taking her girls for the night." Chelsea started to pack the dishes she'd brought into the kitchen into the dishwasher.

"I can do that, Cat." Chelsea felt bad that her friends were running around doing the things she, as the host, should be doing.

"It's not a problem at all," Cat assured her. "Besides, there is a stack of dishes out there, so you'll need to get them through in loads. The quicker we start them the sooner it's done, and you can go get some rest."

"I don't think I'll sleep much for a while." Chelsea drew in a shaky breath. "Does this hole inside you ever fill up?" Her watery eyes looked from Cat to Ashley.

"It heals, and becomes less raw," Cat told her. Cat's eyes darkened with pain for a few seconds.

"Eventually it becomes a part of you, filled with all the memories of the one who made it," Ashley said softly. "And the pain does become easier to live with each day."

"I could always rely on the two of you to never sugarcoat things for me." Chelsea gave a small laugh.

"I found that the flowery words were just that, flowery. They soon wilted and died, leaving nothing but a withered piece of mulch," Cat explained. "But the words that rang with the truth and were at first hard to swallow are the ones that get you through."

"That's weird logic," Chelsea gave a brittle laugh. "But I think I can see the point."

"We're all here for you," Cat told Chelsea. "I know that seems like little comfort because nothing can replace what you've lost. But it gives you a little extra strength and support."

"Thank you, Cat," Chelsea swallowed down the tears burning at the back of her eyes. "Do you mind attending to the guests for another few minutes? I need to go to the bathroom."

"You go," Cat told her. "Ashley and I have got this."

Chelsea gave them a grateful smile before slipping up the stairs that led from the kitchen to the upstairs of the house. She walked straight into her bedroom and made sure no one was in there before locking the door and collapsing in a heap on her bed. Chelsea needed a few minutes to catch her breath. Just a few minutes. She pulled a pillow over her head and closed her eyes for a few seconds, letting her mind drift. Chelsea was still in shock from her mother's death, so she hadn't quite yet processed the fact that Cat was suddenly back in her life.

There was a time when she, Cat, and Ashley had been inseparable. Cat's family and Chelsea's family were supposed to be in some age-old feud that they didn't quite understand so reckoned it didn't apply to them. Her grandparents had been outraged that Chelsea was best friends with a Sparrow. Luckily none of her grandparents were around to have seen Chelsea marry a Sparrow. They would've had something to gloat at though when the marriage had ended. Just like her friendship with Cat had when they were sixteen. Many times after that, Chelsea could picture her grandparents saying 'We told you those Sparrows were no good.'

The truth was that there was nothing wrong with the Sparrow family. In fact, out of all the five families that bordered the Sparrow ranch, Cupids Bow, they were the most special. It didn't matter to the Sparrows if they were angry with you or not. If you needed a helping hand, they were there, complete with everything you needed. They also never asked for anything in return. Callum Sparrow had lived by the rules of his forefathers.

You never turned your back on someone in need, no matter your feelings towards them. When you helped someone, you did it because it was the right thing to do; not because you wanted something in return.

Chelsea smiled to herself remembering Callum's words about lending.

Sparrows don't lend anything we give with a free and open heart. Lending is a muddy slope into an empty well where you keep hoping for that rainy day to fill it. But even when the rain comes, there's never enough to fill it up. So, you're left sloshing in the mud and sinking deeper in.

Chelsea sighed thinking just how right his words were. She

was so deep in that sloshy mud at the moment and there was no sign of rain anytime soon. Chelsea knew she was going to have to face that heap of bills and decided what she was going to do sooner or later. She just didn't want to think about it right now, because it would mean she'd have to sell some of the ranch's assets and Chelsea was attached to each one of them. Especially her beloved horses and cattle. Although she really didn't want to, Chelsea knew she may have to turn to her ex-husband, Zac Sparrow, for help. If it meant not losing the ranch and everything on it, then she'd put her pride in her pocket and do it. Chelsea had made a promise to her mother that she'd make sure the ranch stayed in the family for generations to come. Just like it always had been.

Chelsea knew now wasn't the time to be thinking about the trouble the ranch was in, but for the few minutes she was stressing over it, she wasn't thinking about her mother. Even though she hated paperwork, if it took her mind off her pain and grief, she'd do it. Chelsea moved the pillow off her face and looked at her wristwatch. To her surprise, she'd been lying on her bed for almost ten minutes already. She closed her eyes and took a deep breath knowing that she couldn't be rude and pretend everyone had gone. Chelsea sat up, slid off her comfortable bed, and walked into her bathroom. She looked in the mirror.

"Good grief, Chelsea, you look like a wreck!" Chelsea said to her reflection.

She took out her make-up kit and refreshed her make-up before turning and leaving her room to face the family and friends waiting for her downstairs once again.

Zac Sparrow was sad that he hadn't gotten to say goodbye to Debbie Hitchin. She'd been so supportive of him when Chelsea had walked out on their marriage. He took his share of the responsibility for their marriage ending. Zac also knew that he was the one that had caused the trouble in the first place. He closed his eyes and shook his head, remembering how stupid he was back then. A momentary lapse in judgment and his whole life was turned upside down and his marriage had split at the seams. It was much like the decision he'd made when his sister Cat had left home when she was eighteen. His mother had always told him not to waste his time on should-haves because they were just regrets wrapped in some excuse to justify one's behavior.

Moments like these when you realize that you will never see someone ever again, you can't help but reflect on what you could've done differently. The death of a loved one is always a huge wake-up call because it shows just how fragile and precious life was. At least Debbie got to live her life the way she wanted to live it. She'd had a wonderful husband, a remarkable career, and a daughter she doted on. Debbie had even gotten to live to see her grandchildren have children. Zac had visited Debbie two days before his incident. Unfortunately, he'd not been able to see her for the rest of that week because he was bed-bound. Zac had a broken ankle, bruised ribs, and stitches in his head. He had to fight with his doctor, his sister, his children, and his nephew just to be able to come to the funeral. Zac was also being watched like a hawk by those same people at the funeral. He felt like prison guards were watching him in case he made a dash for it.

"Dad," Jamie, his youngest daughter, now an adult, came up to him. "Have you seen mom anywhere?"

"I think I saw her going to her room, but I didn't see her come down," Zac told her. "You can ask your aunt or Ashley where she is."

"I did," Jamie said, shaking her head. "They lied to my face and told me they weren't sure."

"What is up with your Aunt Cat being so friendly with your mother all of a sudden?" Zac watched his sister Cat and her best friend Ashley walk into the living room.

"I'm not sure," Jamie told him honestly. "Mom hasn't been in the best state to ask too many questions lately either."

"I know." Zac gave her a tight smile. "I'm just wondering what your aunt is up to."

"She's your sister, why don't you just ask her?" Jamie suggested. "I must go find mom as people are wanting to leave."

"Your brother tells me that your mother's freezer is stocked up for a good few months to come," Zac gave a small laugh. "I remember at both my parents' funerals all the food people brought."

"I guess it's nice of them," Jamie said. "I'm just glad this day is over." She shook her head. "It's just too soon after..." Her voice caught in her throat.

"I know, my love," Zac soothed, rubbing her arm. "I would hug you, but I can't with these darn crutches!"

"I know, Dad," Jamie laughed. "See, you always cheer me up."

"It's taken me days to get the hang of these things," Zac told her. "Both my doctor and Liam said if I didn't master them then I couldn't come here."

"I heard about your struggles, Dad," Jamie stepped forward and gave him a hug. "There, now you've had a hug."

"The hug was more to console you than me," Zac told her, ignoring the pain that shot up his leg because he'd had to put pressure on it to balance. Hugging his baby girl was well worth the pain.

"Well, now we're both consoled," Jamie grinned. "I have to go find mom. The Fergusons want to go home and they're old, so we'd better not keep them waiting."

"Jamie!" Chelsea's voice made her jump and spin around. "Don't be rude. They are only about fifteen years older than me."

"That's old!" Hayden said, walking up behind them. "Mom, what else can I do to help?"

"Nothing, honey," Chelsea turned and smiled at her eldest child. "I've got this under control if you and Ruth want to take the kids home."

"Thanks, mom," Hayden kissed her cheek. "It's nearly Gideon and Freya's bath time."

"Please, go look in the freezer and take whatever you and Ruth want," Chelsea told him.

"Thanks, I will do that," Hayden said, hugging her. "Are you going to be okay?"

"I'm staying here with the kids tonight," Jamie told her older brother.

"Yes, honey, I'll be fine," Chelsea gave her son the best smile she could muster.

Zac was worried about Chelsea. She and her mother were very close. Chelsea looked like she hadn't gotten a lot of sleep these past few days. But it was no longer his place to say anything or do anything other than offer her support.

"If you need anything, Chelsea, just let me know," Zac told her.

"Thanks, I appreciate that," Chelsea told him. "If you'll excuse me, I'd better go and say goodbye to the guests."

"Yes, they all want to leave, thank goodness," Jamie breathed a sigh of relief. "I know they all mean well and it's awesome to see how much Gran was loved. But enough is enough."

"I'm glad you said that before I had to," Zac smiled at his daughter. "I'd best go find Liam and Indy, they're taking me home."

"You'll be back on your feet in another few weeks, Dad," Hayden assured his father. "If you'll excuse me, I need to go find Ruth, have a quick shop in mom's freezer, then round up the twins."

"Yes, and I want to go find out where my two are," Jamie's eyes scanned the room. "They've been far too quiet."

"Okay, I'll come say goodbye to my granddaughters before I go," Zac promised. "Especially since I won't see them like I usually do in the morning now that you're staying here for a while."

"It's only for a week, Dad," Jamie laughed and kissed him on the cheek. "Come find me before you go," she reminded him and went to find her two daughters.

Zac needed to find Liam and Indy. His ankle was starting to

ache, and his ribs felt even more bruised from the crutches, just like Liam said they would. But Zac had been determined to be here today and nothing was going to stop him. He stood with difficulty, watching Chelsea put on her fakest smile as she chatted to her guests. Zac could remember doing that at both his mother's and father's funerals. It was hell having to be polite and accept all their condolences. You knew the people there were only trying to show their respect. The only way they could show their support was with food and condolences. But none of those things helped when you're hurting over a death. It was a wound you couldn't see. The pain went deeper than a flesh wound and stayed around for the rest of your life. Your heart was bleeding with emotion, draining your soul, leaving it weak, bruised, and missing a part of it. A part that can never be replaced.

Zac shook himself out of his morbid thoughts when he spotted his sister walking toward him.

"Are you okay?" Cat asked him. "You're looking a little gray."

"I was trying to find Indy and Liam. They are taking me home," Zac told her, frowning.

"What's with that look?" Cat asked him.

"What look?" Zac countered.

"Your judgy look," Cat told him. "You've been giving it to me the entire day."

"I think you're a little paranoid, little sister," Zac told her. "But I have been wondering what is going on with you and Chelsea?" His eyes narrowed. "Are you now best friends again?"

"Why do you want to come between us again?" Cat said sarcastically.

"I never came between the two of you!" Zac hissed. "I couldn't help falling in love with your best friend."

"It's water under the bridge, Zac," Cat told him, with a shrug. "I've moved on."

"Yes, all the way to Nashville," Zac pointed out. "Where you stayed for thirty-one years."

"I told you I would never set foot on Cupids Bow Ranch as

long as the step-monster, Winnie, lived there," Cat reminded him.

"It didn't have to come to that, Cat," Zac sighed.

"Well, it did," Cat said. "And you chose her side, so you pretty much showed me where you stood."

"That's not true." Zac shook his head.

"Really, well from where I was standing it looked like you did." Cat raised her eyebrows. "You had no right to do what you did, Zac. Cupids Bow didn't belong to you or Winnie."

"Cat, she also lost dad, you know." Zac knew he'd hurt his sister back then. Once again those were one of the choices he wished he could make again. "I also needed to follow Dad's wishes. He had wanted Winnie to be taken care of."

"He left Winnie nicely provided for." Cat's eyes flashed with anger. "She could've bought a nice house anywhere in America where she and her horrid sister could stay."

"I see you're never going to see reason on this, are you?" Zac sighed. "Cupids Bow was Winnie's home too, Cat. She had every right to have her sister there."

"No, she did not," Cat disagreed. She held up her hands. "You know what. It's done now, more water under the bridge. Besides, now is not the time to be rehashing old arguments."

"You're right." Zac nodded. "But, Kitty Cat, we really need to talk about this."

"No, we don't," Cat shook her head. "You learned the hard way that I was right. So, I'm good with it. The only thing I'm not good with was you dipping into my college fund to pay the step monster off in the end."

"I put every cent of that back," Zac pointed out. "It was not like you were going to use it anyway. In fact, you never touched it. You used your money from your record deals to pay for your college."

"So that made it alright for you to dip into?" Cat glared at him. She stopped and held up her hands again. "You know what, I don't really care anymore. It was a long time ago." She looked around the room. "I have to help Chelsea clean up."

Cat turned to walk away but Zac grabbed her wrist, nearly toppling himself over when he lost his balance on his crutch.

"Be careful!" Cat spun around and steadied him.

"For what it's worth, I am sorry about everything, Kitty Cat," Zac said softly. "The last thing I wanted was for you to feel like you were being pushed out of your home."

"Don't worry about it," Cat told him. He saw something flash in her eyes before she said, "I'll go find Indy for you to take you home."

Cat turned and walked away from Zac before he could say anything else. He watched her walk towards where Maria Parker was standing and had a sip of her wine. Zac couldn't help but feel that Cat was hiding something from him. Just like she had when she left home at eighteen.

"Hey, Uncle Zac, mom tells me you're ready to leave?" Indy, Cat's son, walked up to him. "Liam is coming now, he's just gone to say goodbye to Aunt Chelsea and Aunt Maria."

"Great," Zac said. "Could I ask you to please go and call Jamie to let her know I'm going soon?"

"Of course," Indy said and disappeared.

"You're looking a little tired." David Miller, the Cupids Bow Ranch foreman, came up beside Zac.

"You're about the fiftieth person to tell me that." Zac looked at David.

"Sorry, but you really do look like you're taking strain," David told him.

"I'm going home as soon as Indy and Liam are ready," Zac assured him. He gave David the once over, like any man sousing up his sisters love interest would. Although he wasn't quite sure what kind of interest Cat had in David yet. "I noticed you and Cat are spending a lot of time together lately."

David turned to look at Zac. He was a few inches taller than Zac. His dark hair was greying slightly at the temples giving David a disguised air along with the way he carried himself so confidently. He dressed like any of the cowboys on the ranches around this area and thought that David's look could be defined as ruggedly handsome. Even though the words distinguished, and rugged cowboy seemed to contradict each other. They summed David Miller up perfectly. A diamond in wilds of Montana are what sprung to mind if Zac were to describe David in a few words for a book.

"Cat expressed an interest in the ranch," David explained. "So, I'm taking her around and getting her familiar with it again."

"How is your shoulder?" Zac asked David, noting that he no longer wore his sling. "I can't believe you were shot, on Cupids Bow land too."

"They weren't after me," David told him. "If they were, I would probably be dead."

"I can't explain how grateful I am that you were there to protect Cat." Zac suppressed a shudder.

About a week ago while David was taking Cat to inspect the south fields of Cupids Bow Ranch someone tried to shoot Cat. But David managed to save her and got shot instead. He took two bullets for Cat. But luckily, they were not fatal wounds. Thanks to the help of their one neighbor, Ryan Beckett, and a very brave horse, Pegasus, the shooter was apprehended. The police found out that he was working for a company called Division Four which turned out to be a shell company that the police were still trying to trace. The shooter had orders to get rid of Cat, Zac's sister, but they didn't know why. The shooter told them that he never asked questions, especially when he was paid cash up front.

But one of Ryan's ranch hands was also involved with the shooter and Division Four. He told the police they wanted Cat out of the way so she couldn't bail the ranches out again. Zac couldn't believe someone had put a hit out on his younger sister. This meant that all his suspicions about the trouble in the area being about a land grab was true. An investment company wanted their land and was trying to get it any way they could. Zac and the rest of the ranchers had thought the trouble ended when the main instigator, Ron Hicks was arrested fifteen years ago. But the trouble started again about five years ago. Only this time whoever was causing it wasn't playing around. They had upped their game and were coming after the ranches quite aggressively.

Zac had lost quite a few heads of cattle and two prize horses. There were four ranches that boarded Cupids Bow because of the way the land was laid out. Four Lakes Ranch, Big Valley Ranch, and Double A Ranch were hit hard but had some funds to fall back on. Mountain Rise Ranch, which now belonged to Chelsea, didn't have any capital to fall back on. Zac knew that Chelsea was up to her eyeballs in debt because the ranch had lost nearly all their cattle and six out of twelve of their quarter horses. She had also had a big staff turnover as she had to cut down on wages due to medical bills for her mother. Zac had seen how badly Mountain Rise was in need of annual maintenance. But he knew that Chelsea could hardly afford to keep the lights on, let alone replace her lost livestock or horses.

"Uncle Zac, are you ready to go?" Liam, Maria's son, walked over to Zac.

"I am," Zac told him, stifling a yawn. "I have to admit to being extremely tired."

"Well, you've had a long day and you're not fully recovered yet," Liam pointed out. "So, you need to give yourself a break."

"What I need is to go rest my old bones." Zac laughed. "I have to keep reminding myself I'm almost fifty-three, not thirty-three anymore."

"There's nothing wrong with identifying as a thirty-three-year-old," Liam told him. "I figure it keeps a person's soul young."

"Thank you, Liam," Zac said, hobbling alongside the young man as they made their way to the front door where Chelsea was standing with Hayden and Jamie by her side.

"Are you going home, Dad?" Hayden looked at him hopefully.

"Yes." Zac nodded.

"Would you have space to give Ruth and the twins a ride

home, please?" Hayden asked. "I need to stay behind and help out here after all."

Zac's brow creased. His eyes traveled to Chelsea. Her jaw was set in its stubborn mode, and he knew something was going on. But he was no longer a part of Chelsea's life and knew he had no right to pry.

"Sure, we can," Liam said. "We're in the Cupids Bow shuttle so there's plenty of room."

"Great, I'll go get them," Hayden said before walking off.

"Let me know if there is anything you need, Aunt Chelsea," Liam said, hugging Chelsea. "I'll take Uncle Zac to the car. Please tell Hayden that Indy will show him where we are parked."

"I will go find them," Jamie offered. "Bye Dad, take it easy." She kissed Zac on the cheek before walking after Hayden.

Liam walked to the door where a couple he knew called him, leaving Zac and Chelsea on their own.

"Is everything okay, Chelsea?" Zac asked, worry creasing his brow.

"You know Hayden, he's such a worrier." Chelsea gave Zac a small smile. "But it's nothing to concern yourself with, really."

Zac knew she was lying but he didn't push it. He had a feeling that Chelsea would reach out to him when she was ready to.

"I'm here if you need me, Chelsea," Zac said softly, giving her a kiss on her cheek. "I'm really sorry about Debbie. You know I loved her like a second mother."

"I know." Chelsea nodded. "Thank you for being here today, Zac. I know how hard it was for you with your injuries. It meant a lot to me."

"I was never going to miss this," Zac assured her. "I'd better go." He turned when Liam called him. "Get some sleep."

Chelsea said nothing, but gave him a nod before waving him out the door.

Chapter Two

IN TOO DEEP

The night sky was clear, and stars scattered across the inky black heavens. It was a warm evening, and the night creatures were celebrating it outside Chelsea's study at Mountain Rise Ranch. The window was open, and the gentle breeze teased the curtains making them shudder on their frame as it blew into the room, lit by the low glow for four lamps. Chelsea kept meaning to get the main lightbulb in the study changed but hadn't gotten around to it. She didn't even know where the large step ladder was to get all the way up to the high ceiling was.

Chelsea and her two children, Jamie and Hayden were sitting in the office so they could go over the ranches books as well as the pile of bills that had stacked. She had been so busy taking care of her mother and the ranch that a lot had fallen by the wayside. Like the bills and keeping up the ranch ledgers or scouring the auctions. Plus, one, two, or a hundred other things that she couldn't juggle during the past few years. Chelsea hadn't even had the luxury of being able to delegate or outsource any of the bits. She had also been bleeding money from all the medical costs and livestock losses.

"Mom, how could you let things get so bad?" Hayden stared

at Chelsea in amazement. "I kept asking you if I could help you with the accounting for the ranch."

"I was busy with your grandmother," Chelsea told him. "You know that with running the ranch and looking after her I hardly had time to breathe, let alone keep on top of bills."

"That's why I asked!" Hayden's voice rang with frustration. "Mom, this is bad!" He held up a handful of bills. "Especially when you don't have the funds to cover them."

"What about the money from Gran's practice?" Chelsea asked.

"Mom, you've been using those funds for your everyday living expenses," Hayden pointed out. "You are also down to only four farm hands because of late and missed salary payments."

"I know, but I have been catching up with those when I can," Chelsea said, then sighed. "I know I'm in deep water here, but there must be something I can do."

"I'll go see the bank first thing Monday morning," Hayden told her. "I can put a chunk of my inheritance from Grandad in to see what I can pull from my Sparrow Trust fund."

"No, I don't want you spending your money on this." Chelsea shook her head. "I won't have it. I'll find another way."

"Mom, listen to Hayden." Jamie looked at Chelsea. "We want to help. Mountain Rise is our legacy too."

"I know, and I didn't want to get you both involved in my problems." Chelsea stood up. "I'll go make us some tea."

"Thanks, Mom," Hayden hardly looked up from the pile of bills he was sorting through. "I've already told Ruth that I'll be staying here tonight."

"No, Hayden, you need to go home to your family." Chelsea looked at her son worriedly.

"It's one night, Mom." Hayden looked up at her. "Ruth understands."

"I'm going to make that tea," Chelsea said, knowing she wasn't going to win, and she didn't have the energy to argue.

While Chelsea put the kettle on the stove and teabags into the teapot, her mind wandered over the events of the past few days. She thought about Cat Sparrow and that she never got to ask why Cat came to her house on the day her mother passed away. The days after that had all sped by in a blur of heartache and trying to organize everything for her mother's funeral. Chelsea made a mental note to give Cat a call the next day. She needed to properly thank Cat and David for all their help that day.

The kettle whistled. Chelsea took it off the burner and filled up the teapot. She went to the refrigerator and took out the cherry pie she knew Hayden and Jamie loved. While the tea steeped Chelsea warmed the pie in the microwave oven. Once the tea and pie were ready, Chelsea knew she had no more excuses to hide away in the kitchen. She had to go back into her study and face down her children's disappointment in her. Chelsea wasn't the best bookkeeper, but over the years she'd managed to balance her accounts. Still, in the last two years it had become harder and harder to juggle her job, her mother, the ranch, and so the accounts were put off. Then when she knew she couldn't ignore them anymore it had seemed like a mountain of debt had piled up.

Chelsea took a deep breath and stepped into the study with the tray, which she put on the small table near the window. "Come get some tea and pie before it gets cold."

"Would you mind doing mine for me please?" Hayden glanced up. He was on his laptop, punching in figures as he neatly stacked bills, letters, and other documents into piles. "I don't want to stop right now."

"I'll do it." Jamie stood up and walked over to her mother. "Why don't you go have a nice hot bath and see if you can get some sleep?" She smiled at Chelsea. "Hayden and I are fine sorting this out on our own." She turned and glared at her brother. "Aren't we, Hayden?"

"Yes." Hayden looked up and smiled at Chelsea. "Mom, you look exhausted. Go and relax. Jamie and I have got this."

"If you're sure?" Chelsea looked from Jamie to Hayden.

"Of course," Jamie started to gently guide Chelsea from the room. "We'll be fine."

"Don't eat all the pie because it will upset your stomach, Hayden," Chelsea warned her son.

"I'll make sure he doesn't," Jamie promised, kissing her mom on the cheek. "Now go, get some sleep."

Chelsea gave Jamie a hug before turning and walking up the stairs to her bedroom, secretly relieved and wanting nothing more than to be alone with her thoughts.

Chelsea didn't feel like a long bath. She was exhausted. So, she had a shower and then headed for bed. As she lay in the dark and closed her eyes, thoughts of her childhood and childhood friends filled her mind.

THIRTY-THREE YEARS AGO - CHELSEA'S STORY

"Happy seventeenth birthday, Chelsea!" Cat Sparrow and Ashley Cuthbert ambushed Chelsea as she walked into her bedroom, nearly giving her a heart attack.

"Oh, wow!" Chelsea grinned, looking around her decorated bedroom. "You did all this?"

Chelsea looked at her two best friends. Cat was tall, slender, and moved like a ballerina. Her hair was a golden-brown and when it was loose dropped down to her lower back. Chelsea had always loved Cat's thick, soft hair that always shone. It reminded her of the mane of a wild horse. She was always stunningly beautiful with high cheekbones, perfect soft pink bow lips, and big aquamarine eyes that were framed by thick long dark lashes.

Ashley was at least a head shorter than both Chelsea and Cat, who were nearly the same height and build. Although she wasn't fat, Ashely had a lovely curvy figure that any woman would want. They teased her that she looked a lot like Marilyn Monroe complete with white-blonde hair that was darkening the older she got. Her pretty face was complimented with rosy, pink cheeks, full lips, and big smoky blue eyes that had a tilt to them making her look more exotic than Marilyn did.

There were time Chelsea felt a little plain compared to the two of them with her mousy brown, wavy hair, and pert nose. She even had an irritating smattering of freckles that ran across her cheeks joining on top of that pert nose. If Chelsea could change anything about her face, she'd want fuller lips because she felt hers were a bit too thin. Her one facial feature she had that her friends wanted were her two deep dimples in each of her cheeks.

"Your mother helped," Cat admitted.

"When you said you didn't want a party this year we got together with your mother and decided to throw you an intimate gathering for your birthday," Ashley grinned.

It was so nice to see Ashley actually giving a full toothy smile again now that her braces had come off. Her teeth looked amazing.

"Are you staring at my teeth again?" Ashley's cheeks flushed, and she shook her head. "You're making me feel more self-conscious about them than when I had the braces!"

"We all had to wear them, Ash," Cat said to her. "Don't worry, you both kept staring at my teeth when my braces came off if you remember."

"That's true," Ashley's eyes narrowed thoughtfully.

"I'm sorry, Ash, but your teeth look simply amazing!" Chelsea walked into her room, plopped down on her bed, and pulled her riding boots off. "For the record, you both kept staring at me as well when my braces came off." She stood up and walked towards her bathroom, "I'm just going to jump into the shower and change quickly."

Chelsea had just come back from her morning ride. On the weekends, she always got up early to go riding. Today her father let her take out his new quarter horse and it was amazing. She'd felt like she was flying across the land on the back of Grandeur. He was big and loved to run. He was also as fast as the wind. Chelsea had gone to the bridge to meet up with her secret boyfriend. They had only been dating for six months, but Chelsea had been in love with him for a lot longer than that. He'd approached her eleven months ago at Cat's sweet sixteen birthday party. They'd danced, flirted, and laughed that night. He was three years older than her, and she'd known him all her life. But he was only there for a few days and had come home especially for Cat's birthday.

Now, he was home for an indefinite time because of an injury. They'd run into each other down by the creek when he was out trying to get some exercise. He'd asked if he could meet her the next day, and they'd met there every day at the same time since. Six months ago, he'd admitted how he felt about her, and Chelsea had been over the moon. Her first thought was to rush over to Cat's house gathering Ashley along the way to tell her two best friends. But she knew she couldn't do that and so they'd decided to keep their relationship between them for now. When the time was right Chelsea was going to tell her two best friends.

Guilt clawed at Chelsea's stomach as she stepped into the shower and let the water wash over her. She knew she'd have to come clean and tell her two best friends about him sooner or later. Chelsea had no doubt that when her two best friends found out about it there was going to be some turmoil about it. Chelsea had broken one of the golden friendship rules and she felt terrible about it. In fact, she'd had many sleepless nights guilting over it since her new love relationship had started. But they had been eight when the three best friends had drawn up their golden friendship rules.

Even back then Chelsea knew in her heart that the rule would one day come back to haunt her. She'd always been fascinated by her new boyfriend. He was everything a girl could want in a boyfriend. Kind, caring, a gentleman, strong, and so very handsome. Chelsea sighed, turning off the water, and wrapping her wet hair in a towel before drying herself. She walked into her dressing room and pulled on jeans and a T-shirt. Chelsea couldn't find her sneakers and went through to her room.

"Have any of you seen my sneakers?" Chelsea knelt on the floor and looked under her bed. "Shoot, where are they?"

She stood up and started to walk out of the room to go look downstairs by the back door, but Cat and Ashley stopped her.

"Wait!" They ran to her and pulled her back into the bedroom.

"Open the present from myself and Ashley before you go in search of your sneakers." Cat's eyes sparkled with excitement.

"We think you're going to love what we got you." Ashley clapped her hands together excitedly.

"Okay." Chelsea's eyes narrowed suspiciously. "What did the two of you do?" She looked from Cat to Ashley.

"Open your present," Cat said impatiently.

"Okay!" Chelsea laughed, taking the gift wrapped in bright paper with a gold bow.

Chelsea opened the present and her eyes widened in surprise.

"Do you like them?" Cat asked her.

"They're the sneakers I've been admiring at the Billings shopping complex." Chelsea looked up at her friends, speechless. "These must cost you both your full allowances."

"Don't you worry about it." Ashley laughed. "Cat and I worked out a plan of how we were going to buy them for you."

"Of course, you did." Chelsea smiled at Ashley.

Chelsea stood up and gave them both a hug.

"Try them on," Cat encouraged her eagerly.

"I just want to get my new socks," Chelsea told them. "Wearing the old grungy ones doesn't feel fitting for my new sneakers."

Chelsea opened her dresser drawer and pulled out a new pair of socks. The color of the socks also matched her new sneakers. After pulling on the socks, she put her new sneakers on, and they fit her perfectly. She knew they would. Her friends knew her so well, just like she knew them. There wasn't anything they didn't know about each other. Guilt once again washed over

Chelsea. That statement about no secrets between the three of them was no longer true because Chelsea was keeping a huge one from them. But today was not the day to expose her secret to them. Today was her birthday and they were going to Billings where they were going to stay the night.

"Are you ready to go to Billings?" Cat asked. "We've already packed the car and your mom said she's ready to go whenever you are."

"Okay, give me a few minutes to finish packing," Chelsea said, pulling on her socks so she could put her new sneakers on. "I've been looking forward to this the whole week."

"So have we," Ashley exclaimed. "We are going to go to the mall, see a movie, have lunch, and then tonight we're dining at an exclusive restaurant."

"Ash, you sound like you've never dined at a restaurant before." Chelsea laughed at her excited friend.

"Not a five-star continental one!" Ashley told them.

"You're right, I don't think any of us have." Cat smiled. "Have you thought about the movie you want to go see?" She looked at Chelsea.

"I'm still trying to decide between the new Indiana Jones movie and Back to the Future Two," Chelsea admitted.

"Oh, please say Indiana Jones." Ashley looked hopefully at Chelsea.

"You and Indiana Jones." Cat shook her head at Ashley. "How many times have you seen the other..." She frowned. "How many of those movies have there been?"

"Two, this is the third one," Ashley informed Cat. "Indiana Jones and the Last Crusade."

"Hopefully it's the last movie!" Cat rolled her eyes and then ducked when Ashley threw a cushion at her.

"I don't mock your movie choices," Ashley said.

"Okay, let's go see the Indiana Jones movie," Chelsea decided.

"Really?" Cat and Ashley said at the same time. Only Cat's face was one of horror while Ashley's was one of delight.

"Yup!" Chelsea said. "We can see Back to the Future Two on your birthday in two weeks' time."

"Oh... right!" Cat nodded. "I'm not sure my dad is going to be able to take us to Billings though."

"That's okay." Ashley patted Cat's arm comfortingly. "Holly said she'd take us if your father couldn't."

"She did?" Cat's eyes lit up. "Okay, Indiana Jones it is today then."

Holly was Ashley's stepmother. She'd been Cat's late mother's best friend since they were very young, just like the three of them had been. Another wave of guilt washed over Chelsea as her secret started to gnaw away at her once again.

"I'm ready," Chelsea stuffed the last item of clothes she wanted to take with them into her duffel bag and slung it over her shoulder.

"Let's go," Ashley was the first out of the door.

ↀ

The road trip to Billings took two hours, and it was always fun when traveling with her best friends. They sang, played road games, and always had a good laugh. Chelsea's mom was also the best. She sang along, played games, and had a good laugh right along with them. Chelsea's mom was even coming with them to the movies. Debbie Hitchin had taken the weekend off from being a surgeon for this road trip, and that meant a lot to Chelsea.

Chelsea had been so lucky to have the parents she had. Her dad was a general practitioner and was a partner at the local clinic in Lewistown. They were both so supportive of her. Even though Sparrows and Hitchins weren't supposed to be friends, her parents encouraged Chelsea's friendship with Cat. Her grandparents, on the other hand...Chelsea rolled her eyes thinking about them. They were never rude to Cat, but you could feel the chill in the air whenever they came to visit and Cat was around that they didn't like her.

Chelsea gave a small sigh thinking how they'd react if they knew about her relationship. They frowned upon dating before the age of eighteen. Her grandparents would be horrified to know she was dating a boy from one of the feuding families. Neither her grandparents nor her parents had ever told her what this feud with the five neighboring families was about. All Chelsea or any of the other children her age from those families didn't have a clue. Chelsea often wondered if her grandparents or parents even knew what it was all about. Their generation had a different outlook on life. If your parents told you not to associate with someone, you didn't. Chelsea's generation saw the world from a whole different point of view.

"We're here!" Debbie told them and was rewarded with a chorus of 'yays'. "Now I've just got to find our hotel."

It didn't take Chelsea's mother long to find their hotel and they were all checked into their suite at the Sheraton Billings Hotel within an hour. Once they'd settled in and changed their clothes Debbie took them to the Rimrock Mall. The first thing they did when they got there was booking their movie tickets. While they waited for their movie they went shopping. Chelsea's seventeenth birthday had started as one of the best birthdays of her life. Little did she know that it wasn't going to end that way. As Chelsea and her friends had a fabulous Saturday, Chelsea never saw fate step in her way to pierce Karma's knife through her heart. The end of her seventeenth birthday weekend would also mark the end of a lifelong friendship.

On Sunday before they left to go back to Lewistown Chelsea's mother, Debbie, wanted to go visit a sick friend of hers that lived in Billings. Her friend lived in an apartment in the city center, so Debbie allowed Cat and Chelsea to go explore the city. Ashley had a dreadful headache, so Debbie had decided Ashley should stay with her. So, Chelsea and Cat set off to explore. They'd just come out of one of Billing's oldest ice cream shops that made the most delicious ice cream when they bumped into Harris Conway. He and his parents had moved to Lewistown four months ago. Harris was in their class at school and Cat had a giant crush on him. Chelsea and Ashley were both convinced that Harris felt the same about Cat because he seemed to always find some excuse to talk to Cat. But about a week ago Chelsea had found out that wasn't the case. Harris was trying to get to know Chelsea through Cat because he wanted to ask Chelsea out. Chelsea had known it was wrong, but she'd been so flattered that the school's newest heartthrob wanted to ask her out. She'd gone on a secret date with Harris. Chelsea knew there was no excuse for what she'd done.

Cat Sparrow was not only talented and brilliant she was also gorgeous. Not that Cat would ever acknowledge it. Cat actually got embarrassed when people said anything about her looks. She looked just like her mother, who was also once the Lewistown beauty. Chelsea and Ashley were also attractive by any standard, but they were always in Cat's shadow. So, for someone to want to ask her out instead of Cat had stroked a hidden ego that Chelsea didn't even think she possessed.

During the date, Chelsea had come clean and told Harris that Cat should be the one he asked out. She also told him that she had a boyfriend and that she shouldn't even have accepted his invitation. Chelsea had thought she'd put Harris off after telling him the truth. She'd been shocked when Harris had told her that he'd win her over because she was the girl of his dreams. That awful feeling of guilt intensified two-fold now and punched her in the stomach. Chelsea couldn't even duck or hide them from him because they'd nearly plowed him over when they barreled out of the ice cream shop. They were now late to meet her mother at the allocated meeting spot.

"Chelsea!" Harris's eyes lit up when he saw her.

"Hi, Harris," Cat's face split into a smile the moment she saw him.

"Hi, Cat," Harris greeted her with a smile. "What are the two of you doing in Billings?"

"It's Chelsea's birthday weekend," Cat explained.

"Oh?" Harris looked at Chelsea with a lopsided smile.

Chelsea and Harris's eyes met and held. Her heart started to thump in her chest and her throat suddenly felt dry.

"Chelsea, your ice cream's melting," Cat said, dabbing at Chelsea's hand with a napkin.

"Oh!" Chelsea looked down to see the pink stain on her yellow shirt. "Aaagh, my mom is going to kill me. This is my new shirt."

"Club soda will get that right out," Harris told her. "I'll let you ladies get on with your day." He stepped out of their way. "I'll see you at school on Monday."

Cat's cheeks went red as she smiled shyly at Harris. He gave them a polite nod and then walked into the ice cream shop. As Chelsea and Cat started to make their way to the meeting point Chelsea realized she'd left her purse in the shop.

"Oh shoot, I think I left my purse in the ice cream shop," Chelsea felt her heart drop. The cold necklace with a heart pendant and inscription on it from her boyfriend was in it.

"You go back and get it, I'll go meet your mother," Cat suggested.

"Okay," Chelsea nodded, turning, and walking briskly back to the ice cream shop.

Before she could go into the shop, Harris came out carrying her purse and he was the one to nearly knock her over this time. Chelsea stopped just in time, but his hand still snuck out and caught her.

"I'm so sorry," Harris said. "I saw your purse and was coming to catch you."

"How did you know it was mine?" Chelsea asked him.

"It's the one you brought on our date last week," Harris told her.

"Excuse me?" Cat's voice sounded like a gunshot behind her, and it may as well have been. Because that incident was the start of their friendship being ripped apart.

"Cat!" Chelsea spun around. Her heart was pounding in her ears before sinking to her feet.

"You went on a date with Harris?" Cat looked at her in astonishment.

"Wait, Cat," Harris stepped up next to Chelsea. "Please, I know Chelsea is dating your brother..."

"WHAT?" Cat's eyes widened further and her face paled as she stared in shock at Chelsea for a few minutes.

"Cat," Chelsea held up her hands. "I can explain."

"Really?" Cat's eyes narrowed, flickering with hurt, anger, and betrayal. "I came back to give you the card key." She shoved it at Chelsea. "Your mother said you must go up to flat number two, two, four when you get to the building."

Cat turned and stormed off, leaving Chelsea reeling.

"Chelsea, I'm so sorry," Harris said to her.

Chelsea knew he probably never meant to blow up her life like he had just done. But he had and Chelsea knew she was in the wrong. That she had hurt and betrayed her best friend but at that moment she needed someone to vent on and Harris was right there.

"Why on earth would you blurt all that out?" Chelsea glared at him. "Stay away from me!"

"Chelsea, wait!" Harris tried to touch her, but she recoiled and stared at him like she was looking at a rattlesnake.

"Don't!" Chelsea held up her hands warding him off before snatching her purse from him. "Stay away from me!" She hissed once again before spinning around and running after Cat.

Cat didn't say another word to Chelsea, which made the trip home awkward and uncomfortable. When Debbie dropped Cat and Ashley off at Cupids Bow Ranch, Cat thanked Debbie politely for a wonderful weekend. She gave Chelsea a clipped goodbye.

"What's that all about?" Debbie asked Chelsea on the drive to Mountain Rise Ranch.

"Oh, nothing. Cat's got a headache," Chelsea lied. "You know how she gets when she eats too much ice cream."

"She really did dig into my friend's homemade ice cream."

Debbie laughed. "Hadn't you girls just been to the ice cream shop as well?"

"Yes." Chelsea made herself smile and look relaxed so her mother wouldn't realize that all she wanted to do was go to her room, lock her door, and cry her eyes out.

At school the next day, Cat and Ashley gave her the cold shoulder. But Chelsea wasn't going to let them get away without trying to explain.

"Cat, Ashley, please can we talk?" Chelsea cornered them during their free period at school that Monday.

"Is it true, Chelsea?" Ashley's eyes narrowed. "Are you dating Zac?"

"I…" Chelsea swallowed. "I wanted to tell you both," she said honestly. "But I could never find the right time. Zac and I wanted to tell you together."

"That's not cool, Chels," Ashley said softly.

"I know I broke one of our golden rules," Chelsea told them. "But we did write them when we were kids. And trust me this has been eating away at me for months."

"Months?" Ashley's eyes widened. "You've been sneaking around with Zac and keeping this secret from us for months?" She stared at Chelsea in disbelief. "How many months?"

"Six," Chelsea's eyes dropped guiltily to the floor for a few moments.

"Oh, wow!" Ashley's brow creased. "Chels, we don't care that you broke those childish golden rules. What we care about is that you lied to us about it and even pretended to still have a crush on Jake Harrow."

"I know," Chelsea admitted. "I'm so sorry." She looked at Cat who hadn't said one word to her since Sunday.

"We need time," Ashley told her. "How do we ever trust you again?" She shook her head and looked at her wristwatch. "Shoot, I have to get to a student council meeting."

Ashley looked at Cat, "It's okay, Ash." Cat smiled at her. "I need to have a word with Chelsea."

"Okay, but promise me you won't kill each other!" Ashley looked from Cat to Chelsea.

"No, don't be silly." Cat gave a small laugh.

Ashley nodded, then walked out of the room they were sitting in.

"Cat..." Chelsea started to try and explain but Cat cut her off.

"No." Cat held up her hand to stop Chelsea from speaking. "I'm sorry but you don't get to spew out your excuses."

"Cat, please listen to me," Chelsea pleaded. "I love Zac and I'm sorry that I feel for your brother. I never in a million years wanted to hurt or betray you."

"You know, Chelsea, I'm not stupid," Cat told her softly. "I've seen the way you and Zac look at each other. I would never have stood in the way of your relationship."

"Really?" Chelsea's brow furrowed as she looked at Cat in surprise. "You're okay with my relationship with Zac?"

"I would worry about how your grandparents would react to you dating a Sparrow," Cat told her.

"Then why are you so mad at me?" Chelsea asked.

"Do you really have to ask that?" Cat raised her eyebrows. "Chelsea, first you lie to us about who you have a crush on and keep your relationship with my brother a secret." Her voice filled with anger. "And if that wasn't bad enough, you're cheating on my brother with a guy you know I like, and you kept that from us as well."

"I'm not cheating on Zac," Chelsea's heart skipped a beat. "Please, Cat, I'm so sorry about Harris. It was a foolish, vain thing to do. I was flattered to finally have someone like me over you."

Chelsea knew how that sounded the moment it came out of her mouth.

"Oh?" Cat looked like Chelsea had struck her. "What do you mean by that?"

"I..." Chelsea swallowed. "I didn't mean it like it sounded."

"It sounded like you did!" Cat pointed out. "I've never even looked at any guy you've had a crush on. So why on earth would you say something like that?" Her eyes sparked with hurt and anger. "I would really like to know."

"Cat, you've always been the prettiest one in a room or even at school," Chelsea didn't know why she was saying what she was. Maybe she was grasping at straws and looking for something to excuse her behavior. "Every other girl and I around you lives in your shadow."

"Excuse me?" Cat breathed, her cheeks flaming red. "When have I ever flaunted what I look like?" Her eyes narrowed. "If anything, I downplay my looks. I didn't ask to look like I do. And when have I ever made anyone else feel like they're somehow inferior to me?" Her eyes blazed. "You know what I think of the so-called beauty queen group at school."

"I'm sorry," Chelsea was just digging herself deeper into the trouble. "I know, Cat. You're the most down-to-earth person with the kindest, most caring heart."

"Whatever, Chelsea!" Cat's eyes went from blazing to blank which in Chelsea's point of view was even worse. "I wouldn't ever have stood in your way of being happy. Whether it was with my brother, Zac, or even Harris if I knew you liked him."

Chelsea wanted to take Cat's words as meaning there was still hope to mend their friendship but, in her heart, she knew Cat was about to severe it for good. Not only was Cat a good person, but she was a loyal one too.

"But you're seeing both of them," Cat's voice dropped. "I would never have expected you to be someone who cheated on someone they loved."

"Cat..." Chelsea's heart felt like it was being ripped apart and bleeding into her soul. "It's not like that. It was one date with Harris."

"Were you still with Zac when you had that one date?" Cat raised an eyebrow. "Or were the two of you on a break?"

"No," Chelsea frowned, realizing too late the trap she'd just walked into.

"Then that was one date too many," Cat told her. "No matter how you try to spin it, you cheated on Zac. Worse, you lied to me about how Harris felt instead of just telling me the truth about everything."

"I'm so sorry," was all Chelsea could think to say. "What can I do?"

"I don't think there's anything you can say or do," Cat said. Her eyes misting over, she closed them for a few minutes before opening them again. Once again, they were devoid of all emotion. "I'm sorry Chelsea but you really hurt me and now I know how you really feel about me too."

"No!" Chelsea's eyes widened and her voice was raw with emotion. "You are taking what I say wrong."

"I don't think I am," Cat shook her head. "I'm sorry, but I don't think this is something we'll get over any time soon."

"Are you going to tell Zac about Harris?" Chelsea knew it was not the right time to ask the question, but she had to know if she'd ruined another relationship as well.

"That's not my call to make," Cat told her.

"And Ashley?" Chelsea's brow creased. "Does she know about Harris?"

"Again, that wasn't my story to tell her." Cat pushed a lock of hair behind her ear. "She thinks I'm hurt about Zac and you."

"Thank you." Chelsea sighed in relief.

"I didn't do it for you," Cat told her bluntly. "I did it for them." She looked at the wristwatch on her arm. It belonged to her mother. "I have to get to class. I need some help with my science project."

Cat didn't say another word but turned and walked out of the room.

Chelsea's throat burned from the tears she was trying so hard to swallow. Her heart ached and she felt like she was living in some terrible dream. Only she knew it was no dream. Her every fear about dating Zac and then her indiscretion with Harris had come back to stab her in her heart. Chelsea had no one else to blame but herself. She knew that she had just thrown seventeen years of friendship away over her own ego and there was no turning back from that.

Chapter Three

ZAC'S TRAP

PRESENT DAY

Cat Sparrow rode Magenta across the fields towards Cupids Bow Ranch.

Maybe Zac is right, and it's time for me to move into my house on Cupids Bow. Cat mulled it over as she neared the ranch. *It would be nice to be back home.*

Since Cat had been home, she'd realized just how much she'd missed the place. In her heart, she knew a big reason why she'd stayed away all these years was that may never have left again. Just like she'd been thinking of selling her apartment in Nashville and her small ranch in Brentwood. Cat had even contacted a real estate agent in Nashville to find out how the market was and if it was a good time to sell. The agent was super keen to sell Cat's properties for her. But it was just a thought right now. Cat would decide once they'd gotten to the bottom of the trouble that had been going on in the area.

Cat slowed Magenta down as they drew near to the ranch house area and walked her horse towards the stables where she was greeted by Craig, the Cupids Bow Stable manager.

"Can I take Magenta for you?" Craig offered as Cat slid off the horse.

"Yes, please," Cat thanked Craig. "I won't be riding again until I go back to Big Valley later this afternoon."

"No problem," Craig told her. "I'll make sure she's taken care of."

Cat thanked Craig again and left the stables to go to Zac's house. She wasn't sure why she'd been summoned to her brother's house this morning, but she had a hunch. Cat wasn't in the mood for a showdown with Zac, but she knew it was inevitable. Zac hated leaving loose ends, and he figured they had enough loose ends to tie up from thirty-one years ago. But Cat needed information from Zac, so she'd have to muddle through his rehashing of her leaving home way back when.

Cat took a deep breath, knocked, and then entered Zac's house. She frowned. It was awfully quiet. She walked through to the room Zac had been using while he was injured. The door had been closed. Cat knocked, hoping she wasn't waking him up, and then nearly died of fright when his voice came from the stairs.

"Hi, Cat," Zac called to her.

Cat spun around, her heart pounding in her chest, and watched her brother hobble down the stairs with his crutches.

"That's kind of risky, isn't it?" Cat put her purse on an armchair before walking to the staircase. "Especially if you're alone."

"He's not alone," David said from behind Zac. "Morning, Cat."

"Morning." Cat's brow creased further. "Are you staying here now?" She looked past Zac to David.

"Oh, no," David said, waiting patiently for Zac to clear the stairs. "I came here early to go over some of the ranch work with Zac. Which he insisted on doing in the office."

"You went all the way up to the attic office?" Cat looked at Zac as if he'd lost his mind. "Do you want to be off your feet for another month?"

"Oh, come on, Cat." Zac laughed. "I'm getting really good on my crutches. Besides, David was right there with me."

"Yes, I can already picture both of you bedridden with broken bones." Cat shook her head.

"Thanks for the vote of confidence," David said. "On that note, I have to allocate chores to the ranch hands."

"Okay, we'll catch up again later," Zac said to David, who nodded, said his goodbyes, and left.

"Why was I summoned?" Cat asked Zac. "I was going to go into Lewistown because I have some legal business with Ashley to take care of."

"Can you do that this afternoon?" Zac looked at her. "I wanted to take you to your house."

"The one across the street?" Cat asked him.

"Yes," Zac grinned. "I think you're going to like it."

Cat felt guilty. She didn't know he wanted to show her the house he'd built for her that was directly opposite his. Cat didn't have the heart to tell him that she and her bodyguard, Wallace, had already gone to look around the house.

"Okay, but should you be walking around so much with broken bones in your foot?" Cat looked pointedly at his foot, which was in an orthopedic boot.

"No, Liam said it was fine as long as I didn't overdo it," Zac told her. "So come on."

Zac hobbled towards his front door and Cat followed him. She watched him closely as he navigated the front steps then when he hopped up the steps to the house he'd built for her.

"You can stop hovering over me now," Zac told her, taking the keys out of his jeans pocket and opening the front door. "I used some furniture from the main house, and I had Jamie help me buy a few choice pieces for you."

"Oh, Zac, this is beautiful," Cat walked in and looked around. "You designed it like my drawing."

"I did," Zac confirmed. "Dad had taken your design and got an architect to draw it. I gave that drawing to Liam, and he did a few tweaks to it."

"I love it," Cat said. "I'm going to go upstairs." She pointed up the stairs.

"I think I'm going to sit down for a few minutes," Zac hopped over to the sofa and flopped down.

"You do that," Cat told him and went up the stairs.

She was actually quite glad to come back here. Cat could take a look around at her leisure without someone watching her every move. She wanted to get into her room in the Inn to see what she could move from there as well. It wasn't fair that Zac could be renting it out to guests. Cat's room in Cupids Bow Ranch house was the best in the house. It had a balcony, a full bathroom, and a small sitting room. Her father had expanded her room for her when she turned twelve. It was all she'd wanted for her birthday that year was her room redesigned and bigger.

Cat loved her house. She stood on the balcony of the main bedroom, staring out over the ranch with the Snowy Mountains looming in the distance. At that moment, she made up her mind that it was time to move back to Cupids Bow Ranch. Cat was going to phone the realtor as soon as she had a free moment to start the process of selling her other properties.

Cat walked back downstairs and stopped at the bottom when her phone rang.

"Hello?" Cat didn't recognize the number.

"Hello, Cat," the deep voice of her ex-husband, Paul, greeted her. "How are you?"

"Hello, Paul." Cat's voice became icy. "What do you want?"

"Can't I call to say hi and find out how you are?" Paul asked innocently.

"That was the old Paul," Cat told him. "The one that wasn't cheating on me with his brother's wife!"

"Are you always going to throw that in my face?" Paul sighed.

"What do you expect?" Cat asked him, walking back up the stairs so Zac wouldn't hear her. "We no longer have to fight over custody for Indy, although you never did. So that means you want something else."

"I want to come and stay at Cupids Bow Inn for a week to

get away for a while," Paul told her. "But I thought I'd clear it with you first."

"Why?" Cat asked him.

"Because Cupids Bow has a reputation between the stars of being one place on this earth stars can go to for peace and quiet," Paul said.

"No," Cat said. "I mean, why bother to ask me? You've never cared about asking me if you could disrupt my life before."

"Come on, Cat," Paul sighed again. "I'm trying to do the right thing here."

"Are you dying?" Cat asked suspiciously.

"No!" Paul sounded frustrated. "Why would you even ask that?"

"I'm just wondering why you're trying to turn over a new leaf," Cat walked back up to the main bedroom.

"I guess after my third failed marriage, I've realized just how badly I messed up my life," Paul told her. "One of my worst mistakes was leaving you."

"Uh-huh," Cat said with disbelief. "Paul, I can't stop you from coming to Cupids Bow Ranch. Indy will be pleased. But I'm warning you not to get in my way or try to monopolize my time like you always do."

"I won't," Paul promised. "You won't even know I'm there."

"Sure, I won't." Cat sighed. This was all she needed right now. Paul poking around her business. "I have to go."

"I'll see you soon," Paul said goodbye and hung up.

"Cat?" Zac called up the stairs. "Is everything okay?"

"I'm fine." Cat walked out of the bedroom and down the stairs. "That was Paul."

"What did he want?" Zac hobbled back into the lounge and flopped back down onto the sofa he was sitting on when Cat went upstairs.

"To ask me if it was okay for him to come stay at the inn for a few days," Cat told him.

"Here?" Zac looked amazed. "That's quite cheeky of him."

"At least he asked and didn't just show up," Cat pointed out.

"What is Paul up to?" Zac's eyes narrowed. "His third marriage just fell apart and now he's wanting to come visit the ranch knowing you're here."

"Maybe he just wants to come and get some peace at Cupids Bow like he said." Cat shrugged. "Either way, I'm not really bothered."

"Do you want me to turn him away?" Zac looked at her with worry in his eyes.

"No, don't do that," Cat shook her head. "Besides, you don't have the luxury of turning people away right now. I've seen the books, and the ranch needs the cash."

"True," Zac admitted. "But we don't need *his* cash."

"It's okay, Zac, really," Cat assured him. "Besides, Indy might act like he doesn't care, but he does, and it will be nice for him to have Paul here for a few days."

"Fine, but say the word, and Paul's gone," Zac promised her.

"Good to know." Cat laughed. "I want you to be the first to know that I'm thinking of selling up in Nashville and Brentwood to come home."

"Really?" Zac's eyes lit up. "Cat that would be amazing. I take it by coming home, you mean move here, to your new house?"

"Yes," Cat nodded.

"Well, I support that decision one hundred percent," Zac told her.

"Good, because when you're better, you're coming with me to Nashville and Brentwood to help me move." Cat laughed.

"Deal!" Zac smiled at her. "What about your singing career?"

"I don't know." Cat sighed and sat back in the plush armchair. "After witnessing firsthand how fickle fans are," she shook her head, "I don't know if I want that anymore. I think I'm done with my country singing time."

"But your music is incredible, Kitty Cat." Zac frowned. "Why don't we make you a studio right here on Cupids Bow? Remember what you and mom wanted to do?"

"What do you mean?" Cat asked. "Mom and I had loads of big plans. You'll have to narrow it down a bit."

"Yes, you two were such big dreamers." Zac smiled, remembering all the plans Cat and their mom would make. "But I'm talking about the studio for promoting local talent."

"Oh, yes," Cat's eyes lit up as she remembered that. "We wanted to turn the storage building into a studio." She looked at Zac. "That building was perfect because it was already sound-proof and there was also the ..."

"The what?" Zac looked at her curiously.

"Basement!" Cat looked up at Zac. "Where is the basement door for the storage building?"

"I think dad closed that up ages ago," Zac told her. "Why do you ask?"

"Do you think maybe dad stored all the old trunks from the attic in there?" Cat asked Zac.

"I don't think so." Zac shook his head. "Like I said, Dad had it filled in for some reason or other."

"When did he do that?" Cat looked at Zac thoughtfully.

"I'm not sure," Zac said. "But we can look back at the records." His eyes narrowed. "What are you up to, Kitty Cat?"

"Nothing, why?" Cat looked at Zac questioningly.

"It's just a feeling I get," Zac told her. "You've been spending a lot of time with David."

"He's been showing me the ranch and how you've changed the systems," Cat told him, blushing. It wasn't an outright lie, it was skirting around the truth.

"Really?" Zac folded his arms across his chest and raised an eyebrow. That was the same type of look their father gave them when he didn't believe a word they were saying.

"Yes, really," Cat assured him.

"Why were you at Chelsea's the day her mom died?" Zac asked her. "A very reliable source told me that you and David arrived there as her mother died."

"Hm." Cat's eyes narrowed. "Let me guess that source. It was either a ranch hand or their housekeeper."

"Neither," Zac denied. "Don't try to wiggle your way out of

this by doing your talk around the subject until the person forgets what they asked you.”

“I don't do that.” Cat looked at him innocently.

“No, not at all!” Zac said sarcastically. “Come on, Cat, no more secrets. We used to be really close once and you told me nearly everything that went on in your life.”

“I still tell you about my life,” Cat pointed out.

“Yes, but those are choice bits with most of it edited out of redacted,” Zac told her. “I had to find out about Paul through Liam. Not even my own nephew told me about Paul cheating on you. With your second marriage to Marshall hitting the skids, I found out through the tabloids.”

“I'm sorry,” Cat said sincerely. “But you were the second person to know that I'd left him.”

“Yes, after you'd told Maria,” Zac pointed out. “That hurt because I'm your brother. How am I supposed to protect my little sister when I don't even know what's going on in her life?”

“That's very sweet of you, big brother.” Cat smiled. “But I have a bodyguard, lawyer, manager, and PR manager to look after me.”

"That's all business protection," Zac pointed out. "I'm talking about all the personal stuff in between. You know the stuff big brothers do. Like, make sure no one is bullying you, scare off suitors that are not suitable, and so on."

"That's very nineteenth-century of you." Cat laughed. "But thank you, Zac, you did your time taking care of me when I was young."

“A big brother's job is never done.” Zac moved his leg awkwardly. “Could you push that footrest towards me, please?”

"Sure." Cat got up and pushed the footrest near him so he could elevate his leg. "I'd make us some coffee, but I don't think there is any."

"I stocked up on essentials that wouldn't spoil easily when I heard you were returning to Lewistown," Zac told her. "I was really hoping that you would come and stay here."

"It was just easier for me," Cat admitted to him. "My childhood memories of home are filled with sunshine, laughter, and so much love. They are happy memories. But sadly, they are tainted by my last memories of this place." She ran her fingers through her shoulder-length hair. "A storm cloud seemed to loom permanently over the ranch after daddy married Winnie Larson. I don't even know what he saw in that woman."

"Winnie wasn't all that bad," Zac stuck up for their stepmother.

"She's a shrew with a hidden agenda," Cat hissed. "She tormented me every chance she got when yours or daddy's back was turned then acted all sweet when you noticed."

"Cat, you tortured her by telling her that mom was more beautiful than her," Zac reminded Cat. "You know how fragile her ego was. Even though she was Miss Montana."

"I never did that!" Cat said frustratedly. "She was the one who kept telling me that mommy's turn as the town beauty queen expired the moment Winnie moved there."

"She said that to you?" Zac's brow creased. "Why didn't you ever tell me or dad?"

"I tried dozens of times," Cat told him. "But you and dad were too busy listening to her lies about me."

"I'm sorry, Cat," Zac's voice was filled with sorrow. "I can't believe we did that. No wonder you hated her so much that in the end, you left home."

"I left home for a number of reasons, Zac, but she was one of the main reasons,' Cat told him honestly.

"Would you mind telling me the rest of the reasons?" Zac looked at her questioningly. "I have wondered about them all these years as well as why you weren't at my wedding."

"I think you know why I wasn't at your wedding, Zac." Cat frowned. "Didn't Chelsea tell you?"

"I already knew that you and she broke up your friendship because she broke one of your friendship golden rules." Zac shook his head. "Geez, Cat, which was kind of harsh you know."

"Is that what Chelsea told you?" Cat looked at him in amazement and laughed. "That figures."

"No, Chelsea never said a word to me other than, don't worry about it," Zac told her. "I had to drag it out of Ashley."

"Ashley?" Cat gave another laugh. "Yeah, she didn't know everything."

"So, you broke off your friendship with Chelsea because she broke a golden rule or two," Zac recounted. "But you were also keeping secrets from another one of your best friends."

"I didn't tell Ashley everything because I knew if you pressured her too much she'd crack," Cat admitted. "I still do not understand how she became a lawyer. Luckily, she's not a criminal lawyer."

"That's not fair, Ashley's a brilliant lawyer," Zac stuck up for Ashley. "She's done a great job handling all the ranchers' business since taking over her father's practice." He grew serious again. "Didn't you just appoint her your lawyer? I know Maria has asked Ashley to take over Aunt Simone's estate."

"Uh-huh." Cat nodded and said no more on the subject.

Zac's eyes narrowed even more as he eyed Cat out. "Why do I get the feeling there's something else going on here?"

"It's not my story to tell you," Cat said.

"Actually, it is because it's part of the reason you left home thirty-one years ago and now, I want to know." Zac stared at her with his stubborn look that told her he wasn't letting this go.

"Fine." Cat sighed. "It's a long story that started when I was twelve."

"I'm not going anywhere!" Zac gave her a smug smile. "And I've told David that you're not available this morning and your plans were changed until the afternoon."

"You planned this!" Cat accused him.

"Guilty," Zac said honestly. "But, Kitty Cat, we need to clear the air once and for all. We used to be so close."

"This is so like you, Zac." Cat shook her head. "You go on and on about something like a dog with a juicy bone."

"I'm just like dad that way," Zac pointed out. "Daddy never let a problem go unresolved."

"If you remember that's when he and I used to fight the

most," Cat reminded Zac. "What I've learned over the years, Zac, is that people are allowed their secrets."

"As long as those secrets don't have an impact on anyone else," Zac said. "But when they affect others, they need to be heard."

"Are we going to argue about keeping secrets the entire morning or do you want to hear my story?" Cat folded her arms across her chest and stared at him.

"Sorry," Zac held up his hands apologetically. "Please, carry on."

"I think this is going to need coffee and cookies." Cat pushed herself up from the chair. "I'll go make us some quick and then I'll tell you the story."

"Great," Zac smiled. "Can I help?"

"No." Cat shook her head. "I've been dying to get into my new kitchen since I saw it."

"Okay." Zac watched her start to walk to the kitchen. "Like I said, I did get it stocked up just in case you came to stay here instead of at the Parkers' place."

"Thanks," Cat called over her shoulder and walked into the kitchen.

Cat knew this day would come. Zac really was like a dog with a bone when he wanted to know something, and he'd waited thirty-one years to hear her story. She sighed and busied herself making coffee. Cat really didn't feel like pouring her heart out to her brother today but maybe it was best to get it over and done with.

Zac watched Cat walk into the kitchen. He knew she needed time to gather her thoughts. Cat wasn't one for opening up and gushing all her feelings out. She was rather private that way and had been ever since their mother died. That's when Cat had shut down. She started to shut Zac as well as their father and trusted housekeeper, Bessie, out. They'd tried to reach her and although she sort of came back to them there was a big part of her that was still closed off. It has remained that way ever since. Then when their father remarried, Cat retreated into her shell once again. She and their father's new wife didn't see eye to eye. They were always fighting. Now that Zac thought about it after Cat had pointed it out, Cat had always ended up being the one in the wrong. Zac frowned. Maybe they had been taking Winnie's side over Cat. His father had practically begged Zac to try to be nice and welcoming to Winnie. At first, Zac had been just as shocked and upset as Cat had been when their father announced he was getting remarried.

But it had been four years since their mother passed away, and their father had dated Winnie for over a year. Well, that's what they found out after he announced the engagement. That was what probably shocked Zac and Cat the most. Their father had kept his dating a secret from them for a whole year. Especially when their father was always the one to tell them that secrets were the root cause of many failed relationships. Then there he was ruining one of the most sacred relationships of all, the bond between family, by keeping a whopper of one to himself. Zac knew their father had a right to his privacy and Zac wanted him to be happy.

When it came right down to it, Zac had always felt he and Cat had the right to know that their father had found another lady to love. Especially when that lady was about to take the place of their mother to become their father's wife. It affected Zac and Cat's life. At least Zac was out of the house and studying when Callum Sparrow married Winnie Larson. But Cat? She had at least another three to four years at home, living under the same roof as their father and his new bride. Their father could've given her a bit more warning that Cat's entire life was about to be turned upside down. Zac had tried his best to be there for his sister and to keep Winnie feeling welcome because Cat wasn't making it easy for the woman. If Zac looked back, he could see now that Cat was telling the truth when she said it was Winnie that started the fights and picked on Cat.

An argument Zac and Cat had a week before Cat left home came back to him. Zac had come home from the army and was recovering from an injury. Bessie had told him that things were explosive at the ranch between Queen Winnie and Cat. Both Bessie and Cat called Winnie 'Queen Winnie'. They said she liked to lord it over them like a queen. Bessie also disliked Winnie. She said that Winnie treated her like nothing more than a servant. Zac had only noticed that when Winnie's sister, Peggy, had moved in. That had happened six months after their father's death, and it had also been the last straw for Cat. Zac had thought Cat was being a petulant child and had told her as much.

That's when Cat had stormed out and didn't come home for a week. She'd gone to stay with the Cuthberts. When Cat eventually came back to the ranch, she laid down an ultimatum. Either Winnie and her sister left the ranch, or she would. Zac had told her that Winnie leaving wasn't an option. Their father wanted her to be provided for and always have a place at Cupids Bow Ranch. Cat had challenged Zac, asking him if he was sure that's what daddy really wanted or if it was what Winnie and Rupert Cuthbert had come up with. Zac had been outraged that Cat could make up such nonsense. Why on earth would Winnie and Uncle Rupert do such a thing. Winnie loved dad and Uncle Rupert was one of dad's oldest friends.

There had been something burning in his sister's eyes. Something she was holding back and telling Zac. He'd tried to pry it out of her, but she'd closed down completely once again like she had when their mother died. Cat had flounced upstairs and packed her bags. When they saw her again, she was heading for the door, bag over one shoulder, car keys in her hand, and her guitar in the other. Zac had tried to stop her. Cat had once again laid down her ultimatum: either Winnie and her sister left or she would. Zac had tried to reason with Cat. He had told her to come sit down and have a family discussion about what was bothering her.

But Cat had flung it in his face that Winnie was not and

never would be Cat's family. Cat had said that the woman was poison, and he was too blinded by her simpering helpless woman act. Cat had then stormed out and left without a backward glance. Zac had tried for two years to call her. He'd even flown to Nashville, but Cat had refused to see him. She'd not even gone to his wedding. Aunt Simone had always made some excuse for Cat not being around when he was there or not taking his calls. Cat hadn't even invited Zac to his wedding. The only reason he'd gone was that Ashley, Cat's best friend, had taken him as her plus one.

Zac may not have liked Cat's first husband, Paul Lockran, Indy's father, but at least the man had made an effort to get Cat and Zac talking again. That's one of the only reasons Zac tolerated the man because he was the one that mended Zac and Cat's relationship. He knew this talk was probably thirty-one years too late but maybe if they completely cleared the air, he might finally also get some answers.

Zac had finally kicked Winnie and her sister, Peggy, off Cupids Bow Ranch. It turned out that Cat had been right about Peggy not being as sick as Winnie had let on.

Zac sighed knowing that he was going to have to tell Cat that she'd been right about Winnie and her sister Peggy. He was not looking forward to Cat gloating for it. But he knew he deserved it.

"Here we go," Cat pulled Zac from his thoughts, bringing a tray with coffee and cookies on.

Chapter Four

REASONS - PART ONE

THIRTY-FOUR YEARS AGO - CAT'S STORY

Cat was furious. She couldn't believe that her father had dropped a bombshell on them like this. He'd been dating a woman named Winnie Larson for the past year. Cat and her brother hadn't been told a thing about the relationship up until today. The day their father announced his engagement to them.

Cat felt hurt and somehow betrayed. Her father had drilled it into her and Zac that secrets were the root cause of failed relationships. Yet, he'd kept a huge one from them. One that did affect Cat and Zac's lives. The worst thing about this engagement was that they were getting married that weekend. The woman's name was Winnie Larson. Her mother owned the sewing shop in Lewiston. Winnie had been a child beauty queen then gone on to become Miss Montana in her twenties. Their father was a very handsome man in his youth. He still was. When he'd married Cat's and Zac's mother they were known as the best looking couple in Lewistown if not Montana. Their mother was beautiful!

Winnie Larson was nothing compared to Grace Sparrow. Cat

sat on her bed and pulled out her mother's photo album. She turned to the picture of her mother holding newborn Cat in her arms.

"I miss you so much, momma," Cat said to her mother's picture, running her fingers over her mother's face. "Why did you have to leave us?"

Tears welled up in Cat's eyes. She pulled her mother's journal from her drawer. Cat had read all her mother's journals so many times over the last four years she knew them by heart. Grace Sparrow had been a remarkable woman that had gone through so much in her life, yet she was gentle, kind, caring, and filled with compassion. She also always had a smile on her face that warmed a person's heart.

A tear dropped off Cat's cheek and landed on the photo. She wiped it away before lying back on her bed with the photo album and journal as she thought about her mother and father's story.

When Cat's mother was eighteen, she'd won a country singing talent show in Nashville with a song she wrote. It had landed Grace a record deal, and her song had topped the charts for a month. Grace could've gone on to be a huge singing star like her Aunt Simone Clark. But her greedy father decided to marry her off to a tyrant, not even caring that Grace was already engaged to Callum Sparrow. Cat was glad she'd never met her mother's father.

Grace's father was a hateful man and a drunk with a bad gambling habit. Cat's mother's father drank and bet away his family fortune. He'd nearly lost their family ranch, which was on the opposite side of Lewistown to Cupids Bow Ranch. When Grace won the record deal, he'd weaseled his way into being her manager, purely so he could control Grace and her money. He drank and gambled away all of Grace's money. Then in an effort to save his ranch, he forced Grace to marry some wealthy man, who took over the ranch, paying off all the debts. A few months into the forced marriage, Grace and Callum ran away together. Grace's husband chased after them and was killed in a car accident. Callum and Grace married not long after that.

Grace had broken all contact with her father and none of her children had ever met the man. Cat didn't even know if he was still alive, nor did she want to know. Right now, Cat needed to call her great-aunt Simone to ask if she could go live with her in Nashville. Cat was planning on moving there one day to become a country singer anyway. She could finish school there and Aunt Simone could start helping her with her music. Cat would be sixteen in a few months. Her father said she could get her learner's permit to drive. If she started working with Aunt Simone now by the age of sixteen, she could get emancipated. Cat was happy with her plan and was feeling a lot better.

"I'm sorry, momma," Cat said to her mother's photo. "But I don't like the woman that daddy's gotten engaged to." She shook her head. "There is just something about her that I don't trust." She bit her lip thoughtfully. "And before you think it's because I don't want her to replace you..." She sighed. "Okay well, there is that reason. But I don't think her intentions for marrying daddy are good ones."

Cat could hear what her mother would say to that.

Honey, you can't always judge a horse by what it looks like. Remember everyone has been through something in their life. You've got to give them a chance, princess.

"I know, momma." Cat sighed again. "But you also taught me to trust my instincts because you believed I had good ones. Well, momma, my instincts are screaming that there is something sinister about the woman."

Cat gave a brittle laugh, realizing she was doing it again. She was talking to herself. Zac always mocked her for doing it. Momma claimed that Cat had been talking to herself since birth. She'd sometimes get quite a fright because Cat would start giggling out of the blue, as if someone Grace couldn't see had whispered in her ear. But Cat had always processed things better if she voiced them out loud to herself. That's why she loved music so much. She got to sing her feelings and thoughts to a melody that fed her soul. Cat had sung at school and in concerts on stage. Cat loved being up there and singing her heart out getting her audience to connect with her music, flowing with her emotions.

"Cat?" Zac called through her locked bedroom door. "Will you open up?"

"Go away!" Cat yelled. "I want to be left alone. I'm working."

"You don't work!" Zac told her.

"I do!" Cat yelled again. "I write music. That's work for me."

"You're not a singer yet," Zac reminded her. "Come on Kitty Cat, open the door. I have chocolate."

"I won't be bribed," Cat told him. "Besides it's almost dinner time and Bessie will have your hide if you feed me chocolate now."

"We won't tell her!" Zac promised.

"Go away," Cat yelled again. "I don't want to be disturbed. Can't you read?"

"You never take this sign off your door," Zac told her. "It's a permanent fixture."

"That's because when my door is closed, I don't want to be disturbed," Cat explained. "Now go away."

"I'm not going away," Zac warned her. "I'll start singing."

"Go ahead, I need a good laugh." Cat sat up. She quickly shoved her mother's photo album and journal into her bedside table drawer. "Okay, I let you in. But if you don't have chocolate, you're going to be sorry."

"I promise I have chocolate, it's your favorite." Zac rattled the wrapper.

"I'm opening the door." Cat unlocked the door and slid it open a fraction to peak out. "Show the goods, buster."

"Here you go!" Zac handed her the candy bar.

"Fine, you can come inside." Cat pulled the door open, stepped back, and let him in the room.

Cat quickly closed and locked the door behind him.

"No one is going to come in after me, I promise you," Zac tried to assure her.

"I'm not taking any chances," Cat told him and flipped her radio on. "I know no one believes me, but that woman is up to no good."

"Which woman?" Zac asked her, watching her peel open the candy bar and take a bite.

"Winnie Larson," Cat said impatiently. "Keep up, Zac."

"Cat, you've only just met her," Zac pointed out. "Maybe give her a few days' grace before making your snap judgments?"

"I don't need to." Cat shook her head. "All I needed was to see that malicious look in her eyes when she met me."

"I think you're seeing things." Zac sighed and shook his head. "I was right there next to you when we met her, remember?"

"Yes, but you weren't looking when she flashed me her evil eye look," Cat insisted. "That woman is the one who's already made up her mind about me."

"Kitty Cat, most of the female population look at you like that at first!" Zac gave her a smile.

"Why on earth would you say something like that?" Cat frowned.

"Don't you look in the mirror every day," Zac said. "You look just like mom. The older you get the more you look like her and as you know mom was gorgeous."

"Oh, that!" Cat shrugged it off. "You know I'm not hung up on looks and I try my best to not stand out."

"Unfortunately, little sister, for you that's impossible," Zac told her. "Even with your hair scraped back as you wear it and no makeup whatsoever, you can't hide what you look like."

"That's not my fault," Cat said hotly. "I should go to a plastic surgeon and ask him if he can make me look normal."

"I bet that would be a first for the poor surgeon you approach." Zac laughed. "Listen, I'm your brother and I know just how hard I've had to fight guys to keep them away from you."

"That's utter nonsense!" Cat's cheeks flamed. "You know I'm

not interested in relationships at the moment. I have too much to do in my life to be tied down."

"Well, you're not even turned sixteen yet, so give it a few months," Zac assured her. "I think you'll change your mind."

"I doubt it," Cat said. "Besides, why would someone of Winnie's age feel threatened by me? A teenager."

"I think all beauty queens are insecure," Zac shrugged. "They need the world to assure them they are beautiful."

"You only say that because Jenna Shultz dumped you when she won Miss Teenage Montana!" Cat gave him a big smile when he glared at her for reminding him about her.

"She was really insecure about her looks," Zac told Cat. "That's why she hated you so much. She had to work to make sure she looked the prettiest while it just came naturally to you."

"Will you stop with my looks!" Cat hit him with one of her throw cushions. "This is about that woman our father is about to make the worst mistake of his life by marrying."

"Kitty Cat, there's not much we can do about it," Zac pointed out. "We can only support him and be happy that our father found someone to help him heal his hurt from momma's death."

"We're all still hurting over momma's death," Cat reminded him. "What? Are we supposed to find someone to help us heal our souls too?" She raised her eyebrows. "Because I don't think getting over the death of a loved one works that way."

"I tell you what!" Zac bargained with her. "Let's give Winnie a couple of months and then revisit this conversation. If we both feel that she's not right for dad, then we can go speak to him together about our concerns."

"I think we should both go and speak to him about our concerns now," Cat said. "Because he's already been dating Winnie behind our backs for a year!"

"Okay," Zac said, holding up his hands. "We'll talk to dad."

"So, you agree that Winnie is not for dad and is up to something?" Cat looked questioningly at Zac.

"I'm not saying that," Zac replied. "But I'm saying maybe we should get to know her first before welcoming her into our family."

"I'll take that," Cat told him. "Let's go find dad."

"Not now!" Zac looked at her in surprise. "Winnie is still here."

"Get rid of her," Cat said. "Offer to take her home because you have to go get supplies in Lewistown."

"No way am I leaving you here alone with dad," Zac warned her. "If we talk to him about this, we do so together."

"Then I'll come with you when you take Winnie home." Cat looked at him innocently. "You know, to spend more time getting to know her on the twenty-minute drive to Lewistown."

"Oh boy!" Zac sighed, standing up and shaking his head. "Let's go and see if this plan of yours is going to work."

"Sure, it will," Cat grinned. "Dad will think we're being kind and trying to get to know his fiancée."

"Or he'll insist on coming with us," Zac warned her. "Which is what I'd do if I was him."

"Maybe." Cat shrugged. "Then we'll get to have a family outing to Lewistown. Maybe he'll take us out for dinner?"

"You always have a play up your sleeve, don't you?" Zac walked out of Cat's room with her close behind him.

"I thought we were going to have a family dinner," Cat grumbled, sitting at the restaurant in Lewistown with her father, Zac, and Winnie who'd wormed her way into being invited.

"Don't be rude, Kitten," Callum Sparrow said under his breath for his daughter's ears only. "It was nice of Winnie to offer to take us out for dinner."

"Since when do you let a woman pay for your meal?" Cat whispered back.

"You're being offensive," Callum warned his daughter.

"No, I was looking forward to having dinner with my family," Cat raised her voice.

"Cat, I'm warning you." Callum stared at her with his 'I'm about to get angry' look.

"Whatever, dad," Cat said. "You know what, I'm not hungry." She started to slide out of the booth.

"Where are you going, Cathleen?" Callum only ever called Cat by her full name when he was getting angry or exasperated with her.

"To visit Ashley," Cat took her coat and purse from the seat. "I'll ask Uncle Rupert to bring me home tomorrow."

"Cat!" Zac looked at her with a warning light in his eyes. "Don't do this. You're the one that wanted to have dinner in Lewistown."

"Yes, but I wanted to have dinner with *just* my family." Cat's eyes narrowed on the cold glare Winnie was giving her. "Not some stranger who keeps glaring at me." She looked Winnie right in the eyes when she said that. "It made me lose my appetite."

Before anyone could say anything more, Cat spun on her heel and marched out of the restaurant. She didn't stop walking until she was knocking on the Cuthberts' door, which was not too far from the restaurant.

"Why, hello there, young Cat." Rupert Cuthbert answered the knock on their door. "What brings you to town?"

"Oh, you know." Cat looked up at him. "Zac, my father, and some woman he's engaged to."

"Ah." Rupert nodded. "I see."

"Do you?" Cat's eyes narrowed. "You've known about my father and that dreadful woman for some time, haven't you?"

"Well..." Rupert pulled a face and stepped back to let her in. "We are good friends."

"Yes, but you could've given me a heads up." Cat walked into the house. "Where's Ashley?"

"She's up in her room," Rupert told Cat. "Are you staying for dinner?"

"Actually, I'm staying the night if that's okay?" Cat gave him a sweet smile.

"You know you are always welcome in our house," Holly, Rupert's wife, and Ashley's stepmother walked through. She gave Cat a hug. "I want you to know that I also only found out about your father and Winnie a few days ago."

"I don't believe you," Cat said to Holly. "Because you'd have told me!" She gave Rupert a scathing look. "You're supposed to be my guardian."

"Yes, Rupert, that was not nice," Holly admonished her husband. "Especially because you kept me in the dark as well."

"We've already had our fight about this, Holly," Rupert sighed. "How many more times do I have to tell you that I promised my friend I'd keep his secret?"

"Not, cool, Uncle Rupert," Cat said as she walked towards the stairs.

"Did I hear Cat?" Ashley's voice came from the second floor.

Cat looked up the stairs and saw Ashley rushing towards her. "Hey, Ash."

"Hey, Cat." Ashley ran down to Cat and gave her a big hug. "I've just heard about your dad's engagement."

"I know." Cat's eyes sparked with anger. "That woman has wheedled her way into my father's life."

"Winnie Larson!" Ashley rolled her eyes. "That woman is meaner than a rattlesnake."

"Now, ladies!" Rupert warned them. "Winnie is not that bad."

"Not if you like washed-up beauty queens who hate Cat," Ashley pointed out.

"How can you say that?" Rupert asked Ashley. "Winnie doesn't even know Cat."

"When she first moved to town she stopped up in the street and asked Cat if she was Grace Sparrow's daughter," Ashley told her father. "We didn't know who she was, so we told her we don't speak to strangers and tried to walk off."

"But she grabbed my wrist and told me she wasn't a stranger,"

Cat continued the story. "She knew my momma from school and some or other talent competition."

"Then she laughed and said, 'you look just like her, don't ya?'" Ashley picked up the story. "Winnie looked Cat up and down as if she was dirt on her shoe. Then she said, 'your momma thought she was pretty too just like you. But I showed her at that talent show.' then she flounced off laughing."

"She called over her shoulder," Cat continued for Ashley. *"Guess I'll be showing you as well who the prettiest girl in town is."*

"She said that to you?" Holly's eyes widened with shock. "Did you tell your daddy about this, Cat?"

"No," Cat shook her head. "I was going to have what was supposed to be a family dinner at the restaurant when Winnie wheedled her way into that too."

"So that's why you're choosing to eat Holly's roast chicken pie instead of Stew Rowan's gourmet food!" Rupert nodded as realization dawned on him.

"Hey, what's wrong with my roast chicken pie?" Holly put her hands on her hips and glared at Rupert.

"Nothing, my darling," Rupert said, kissing Holly's head. "You make the best chicken pie in the world."

"You truly do, Aunt Holly," Cat assured Holly.

"Besides my pie," Holly looked at Cat worriedly, "you need to tell your daddy what Winnie said to you."

"I will as soon as I get a moment to speak to him," Cat told Holly. "Since we met her and found out that she and daddy are engaged I haven't had a moment of his time."

"Are you a little jealous, Kitty Cat?" Rupert looked at her curiously. "You will always be your daddy's number one girl, you know that!"

"Of course," Cat agreed with Rupert. "But she ain't gonna like that much. She's already trying to wedge her way between daddy and me."

"Rupert, I don't like the way Winnie talked to Cat and Ashley," Holly said indignantly. "That's not right!" She looked at

Cat compassionately. "I'm sorry you had to go through that, Kitten."

"Thank you, Aunt Holly," Cat replied. "But now she's going to try and stop me from telling daddy. Or she'll say I'm lying or something."

"You don't know that, Cat," Rupert told her. "Let's give Winnie a chance to get to know you and Zac before we judge her."

"Now you sound like Zac." Cat rolled her eyes. "But, okay, I guess we can do that. I'm still not going back to the restaurant though."

"You don't have to, love," Holly told her. "Rupert will take a walk over there and tell your daddy that you're with us tonight."

"Thank you, Aunt Holly." Cat gave Holly a hug.

"Now you two run along. I'll give you a shout when dinner is ready," Holly told them. "You, Rupert, can go let Callum know Cat is with us tonight."

"Sure, dear." Rupert sighed, walking over to get his hat and coat. "I wanted to go for a quick walk before dinner anyway."

Ashley and Cat ran up the stairs to Ashley's room as Rupert left the house.

"You shouldn't have told your father and Holly about what Winnie said to us," Cat told Ashley. "I'm sure your father is going to say something to my dad and it's going to cause an upset."

"They needed to know what that woman is really like," Ashley shuddered. "I can't imagine what your father would see in her."

"Love is blind, I guess." Cat shrugged. "But let's not talk about her. We have a trip coming up."

"Oh, yes the school trip to Washington, DC." Ashley's eyes lit up. "I can't wait."

"Neither can I." Cat grinned. "It's going to be my third time on an airplane."

"My first," Ashley admitted. "I'm both excited and nervous about flying."

"I think it's also Chelsea's first time flying," Cat said.

"Yes, it is." Ashley nodded. "I'm glad you came here tonight. I was getting so bored."

"I'm glad I came too." Cat sighed. "I couldn't spend another minute in that woman's company."

"I think you should do what my father suggested and give her a chance," Ashley said. Holding her hand up when she saw that Cat was about to pounce on her. "Then you can find out exactly what she's up to. Because I think it's just a little too coincidental that she said what she did when she first moved here. If your father and she have been dating for a year that means she couldn't have been here long when she met him."

"I never thought of that." Cat frowned and rubbed her chin thoughtfully. "But you're right. That's what I'll do. Now let's talk about the trip to Washington."

Ashley walked to her bookshelf and pulled down all the books she'd bought about Washington.

THREE MONTHS LATER

"Cat, where are you going?" Callum watched his daughter rush to the front door with her bags packed.

"It's the Washing, DC school trip," Cat reminded him. "I've reminded you four times this week already."

"Oh, honey, is that this week?" Callum looked at her wide-eyed.

"Yes, daddy, it is!" Cat's brow creased. "And if we don't leave in a few minutes I'm going to be late for the school bus to Billings."

"But sweety, I'm getting married on Saturday!" Callum said.

"WHAT?" Cat spat. Her heart felt like it had dropped to her feet and shock waves buzzed through her while a red-hot anger started to boil in the pit of her stomach. "I thought that was next month?"

"No, Winnie didn't want to wait any longer," Callum told her. "Honey, I told you this two days ago."

"Oh, no, you didn't!" Cat shook her head, wide-eyed. "You said nothing of the sort to me and I've been on at you about Washington the entire week. You even put money in my account for the trip yesterday."

"Again, I thought that was next week!" Callum said. "I need at least one of my children at my wedding because your brother can't make it. He can't get leave from the military."

"Or he just doesn't want to be there," Cat mumbled beneath her breath. "Well, I'm sorry daddy but I'm not going to be there either. It is also unfair of you to try and stop me from going on this school trip I've been planning for months!"

"Of course, honey." Callum pinched the bridge of his nose. "I'm sorry if I didn't tell you. I really thought I had."

"Is everything okay, Daddy?" Cat asked him worriedly.

"It's fine, Kitten," Callum tried to reassure her. "It's just all this business with the Donaldson's property and the Beckett land being poisoned."

"Cattle's being poisoned on Four Lakes?" Cat asked, shocked. "Daddy, you should get Winnie to move the wedding back to when it was supposed to be so Zac and I can be there."

"Yes, yes, I'll talk to her," Callum told Cat. "You're right. Besides, all the guests already know the date and it would be rude to change their plans."

"Exactly," Cat agreed. "Why is she in such a hurry anyway?"

"She's excited to join our family, Kitten." Callum smiled. "Look, don't you worry about it. Let's get you to that school bus."

"Okay," Cat picked up her purse letting her father take her suitcase as they left the house. "I'm so excited about this trip."

"I'm not, I'm going to miss you," Callum told her.

"It's only for seven days, dad," Cat told him, climbing into his brand new pickup truck.

"That's seven days too long for a parent," Callum said,

climbing into the driver's seat. "Now both you and your brother will be gone."

"You'll have some peace and quiet," Cat pointed out. "We need to pick up Chelsea. Remember you offered to take us, and the Hitchins are going to fetch us when we get back."

"That's right," Callum nodded. "I do remember." He smiled and headed towards Mountain Rise Ranch.

"What is she doing here?" Cat said beneath her breath for only Chelsea and Ashley to hear. They picked the girls up on the way to the school.

"Good grief!" Chelsea shook her head. "You'd think she'd give you this time to say goodbye to your father."

"I can't believe she wanted you to cancel your trip because she wants to get married a few weeks earlier!" Ashley said in disgust. "Have you told your father about your first meeting with Winnie yet?"

"No, I haven't had a moment yet," Cat told her friends. "Every time I turn around, she's there."

"Like a bad penny," Chelsea said, walking around to the back of the pickup with Cat and Ashley.

"Hi, girls," Winnie's voice rang with false cheer and her eyes blazed with anger.

"Hi, Winnie," Callum greeted her. "What are you doing here?"

"I thought I'd come and say goodbye to Cat and her friends," Winnie fluttered her eyelashes prettily at Callum. "We are going to be family soon."

"Yes, we need to talk about that," Callum told her. "But now is not the time. I want to see my daughter and her friends off."

"Of course," Winnie said.

But the woman still didn't back off; she stuck to Callum's side like glue.

"Do you have enough money?" Callum asked Cat and her friends.

"Yes, dad," Cat said, kissing his cheek. "Thank you for bringing us. We have to get on the bus now." She grinned as her father squeezed her.

"Be careful and listen to your teachers and chaperones," Callum advised her.

"We will," Cat promised, wiggling out of his hold.

"Just call me if you run out of money or need anything," Callum told her. "And that goes for Chelsea and Ashley too."

"Thank you, Uncle Callum." Ashley and Chelsea hugged Callum goodbye.

Winnie stepped up to give Cat a hug, but luckily the one teacher ran over to them and interrupted what would've been a rather awkward moment for Cat. Cat stepped away from Winnie.

"We have to run." Cat kissed her father one more time before turning and running to the bus with her two friends, dragging her case behind her.

"Wow, how pushy is Winnie?" Chelsea breathed.

"I know right?" Cat nodded, handing her bag to one of their teachers who was packing the luggage compartment of the bus.

The three girls got on the bus and found their allocated seats. Cat always had the window while Chelsea preferred the aisle putting Ashley in the middle.

"Well, we're getting away from the Winnie madness for an entire week!" Ashley said excitedly. "Washington, DC, here we come!"

Chelsea and Cat cheered along with Ashley and the rest of the students as the bus took off. Cat looked out the window and waved to her father as they drove by him. A shiver slid down her spine at the look Winnie gave her. Cat sat back in her seat as a bad feeling washed over her. She was sure that their life was never going to be the same again once Winnie was embedded permanently in it.

A dark cloud had started to form over Cat's happy life. A life that she'd tried to cling onto since the day her mother died. She also had a feeling that Winnie was somehow connected with the problems the ranches around Cupids Bow had started having. Even Chelsea's family's ranch had been hit with a lot of their cattle being poisoned. Maybe Cat was being cynical and looking for a reason to dislike Winnie but that part of her that somehow just knew things told her she was right. It also screamed at her to tread wearily around the woman because she had a darker side than Cat and her friends had already witnessed.

As the bus pulled onto the motorway towards Billings, Cat swore to find out everything she could about the woman. But for now, she was going to forget about the wicked Winnie witch and enjoy the school trip. Cat and her friends had been looking forward to it for months.

Chapter Five

REASONS - PART TWO

THIRTY-THREE YEARS AGO - CAT'S STORY

"**D**id you see Harris today?" Cat's eye sparkled as she asked Chelsea and Ashley. "He is so handsome."

"I've never seen you like that over any guy!" Ashley laughed. "Wow! Cat's first big crush."

"Well, he is handsome," Chelsea said with a smile. "But he's not the most handsome man in Lewistown."

"Oh?" Cat's shrewd eyes looked at Chelsea, who blushed. "Do you have someone you're crushing on as well?"

"What?" Chelsea looked surprised. "Oh, no. I'm still crushing over Michael J. Fox."

"He's a movie star, Chels." Ashley shook her head. "You can't crush on a movie star. They're unobtainable."

"Not really," Cat said. "I'm sure lots of small-town country girls have married movie stars."

"I guess it could happen." Ashley shrugged. "The probability of it happening is not that high though. Besides, isn't he Canadian?"

"Yes, but I'm sure he lives somewhere in L. A. now," Chelsea told them and sighed.

"Wow, and I thought Cat being anti-relationships until she's eighteen was bad." Ashley shook her head. "But here's Chelsea crushing on a movie star instead of the hundred or so teenage boys who are crushing on her."

"Nah!" Chelsea waved Ashley's observation off. "I'm not interested in some high school boy."

"Okay..." Cat gave Chelsea a curious side-ways look. "We'd better get to gym class."

"Ugh!" Ashley lifted her head and rolled her eyes. She hated gym class. "I'm not as sporty as you two are and I'm not out riding every day either. I'm more of a band geek."

"Yes, you are," Chelsea and Cat said together with a laugh before hugging their friend.

"Ooh, look who's at his locker, Cat." Ashley pointed to Harris Conway. "He's looking this way."

Cat blushed when Harris smiled and waved at the three of them. Cat shyly waved back before they disappeared into the girls' locker rooms to get changed for gym.

PRESENT DAY

Zac looked at Cat with big eyes, "Why are you telling me about your trip to Washington and your crush on Harris Conway?" His eyes narrowed and then widened. "Harris Conway?"

Cat nodded and bit her bottom lip as she watched the emotions run across her brother's face.

"You and Chelsea knew Harris Conway from school?" Zac was looking at her in disbelief. "Harris Conway, who used to once work as the foreman for Cupids Bow and ran off with my ex-wife?"

"Yes, he is one and the same," Cat confirmed.

"Why didn't Chelsea ever tell me she knew him from school?" Zac's brows furrowed.

"I do not know the answer to that question, Zac," Cat said

honestly. "By then, Chelsea and I hadn't been friends for at least ten to fifteen years."

"Of course," Zac nodded. "I know. Sorry, Kitty Cat, I wasn't trying to entrap you into answering that. I doubt I'll ever get an answer from Chelsea as we are divorced so I have no right to ask her."

"I think you do," Cat told him. "You employed the man on false pretenses."

"He had excellent credentials and he used to run his family's farm until he had to sell it," Zac said. "I should've realized Chelsea knew him when she introduced him to me."

"Chelsea introduced Harris to you?" Cat frowned. "Really?"

"Yes." Zac's frown deepened. "Why is there something I should know?"

"Let me finish my story." Cat shook her head and rolled her eyes. "You always do this. Try to jump ahead to the end of a book or movie."

"I tend to get bored with all the bits in-between in books and movies," Zac told her. "I know what's going on in the middle and want to know how the writers will wrap it up."

"Is that what you're hinting at?" Cat laughed. "Because I told you it was going to be a long story with each bit having something significant in it."

"Yes, like when dad first broke step monster Winnie home, her meeting with you and your friends in town, and her coming to your Washington send off." Zac nodded. "I got the point of those. And now your final showdown with Winnie makes a lot more sense to me."

"Okay, so you were listening," Cat laughed.

"Yes, and you also slotted Harris into your story which I assume you were trying to tell me that Chelsea knew him from school?" Zac asked her.

"You're fishing. And I'm going to tell you again that I do not know why Chelsea didn't tell you she knew him," Cat pointed out. "I can only tell you my side of the story and what I know about their early relationship."

"Relationship?" Zac asked her curiously. "What are you trying to tell me?"

"Just listen to the final part of my story." Cat rolled her eyes. "Remember you asked to hear about this."

"I know," Zac said, holding up his hands. "Sorry, please continue."

"Thank you," Cat said.

THIRTY-THREE YEARS AGO - CAT'S STORY CONTINUED

"Do you think Chelsea's been acting strangely these past five months?" Cat asked Ashley. They were in Ashley's bedroom, studying for a science test.

"Now that you mention it, she has." Ashley looked up from the book she had her nose in.

Ashley was sitting at her desk while Cat had taken up a place at Ashley's dressing table. Cat liked to study at Ashley's place because it was quiet. After all, Ashley's parents both worked during the day. Cat liked spending as much time as she could at her friends' places ever since her father married Winnie three months before Cat's sixteenth birthday. That was not a birthday Cat even liked to think about. It was supposed to be her sweet sixteen party, but Winnie had ruined the whole thing by taking it over.

Winnie had canceled the venue Cat had booked and opted for a tacky downtown hall instead. Then she'd not listened when Cat had told her how she wanted to decorate and had swapped Cat's party dress out at the last minute. Instead of the beautiful, elegant blue dress that emphasized her eyes that Cat had bought, she'd changed it for a hideous pink thing. Then Winnie had the gall to make the excuse that the lady at the dress shop must've made the mistake and given her the wrong dress. By then it was too late as the shop was closed so Cat had to wear a dress she borrowed from Chelsea. There was no way she'd ever wear the monstrosity Winnie had tried to make her wear.

Then Winnie had made a scene crying and pretending she was so upset at having ruined Cat's special birthday. That had been all a ruse to get Callum's attention away from Cat for the day. Luckily Cat's two best friends had rushed to her rescue, and they'd tried to fix up the hall as best they could. Chelsea even fired the dumb band Winnie had insisted they hire and got Cat a DJ. Cat had a huge fight with Winnie before they left Cupids Bow Ranch and she told her father that she didn't want Winnie at her party. This of course angered Callum and made Winnie cry, and Cat had ended up asking their housekeeper, Bessie, to take her to her party.

Cat had stormed into the hall and had been so surprised at the transformation her friends had made that she'd nearly burst into tears. She'd soon forgotten the fight with Winnie and her father, but they hadn't. But Callum saw how much fun his daughter was having and to him, birthdays were special days for a person, so he'd let the argument go. Winnie didn't, and she kept bringing it up for the next few days until Cat finally shut her up. She marched Winnie and her father into Lewistown to meet the owner of the dress store, who told Callum that Winnie had, in fact, swapped out the dresses. The owner even had the receipt for the amount she'd refunded Winnie for the hideous pink dress.

That took Winnie's attention off of trying to make Cat's life a misery for a good two weeks while the woman tried to make things right with Callum. There were only a few things that made her father angry; one of them was being a liar, another was spite. What Winnie had done was spiteful and petty as Callum had pointed out. Winnie had tried to tell Callum that she thought the blue dress wasn't appropriate and that the pink one was a lot better. But Callum wasn't a fool and Cat was sure that was the moment where a tiny tear had started in Callum and Winnie's relationship. Her father was finally starting to see what a spiteful shrew Winnie Larson really was.

Of course, Winnie had since retaliated and started to be a lot sneakier about her attacks on Cat. That is the reason why Cat hardly spent a weekend at Cupids Bow these days. She went home after school, spoke to Bessie, did her homework, went riding, had dinner, and then went straight up to her room to bathe and then to bed. Cat hardly spoke to Callum these days either. She was angry at him for bringing that horrible woman into their lives and disappointed that he still took her side whenever she managed to goad Cat. Callum even ignored Bessie when she tried to stick up for Cat. Even Zac who'd now been home for six months after being shot while deployed had started to stick up for the witch. The worst part was that Cat had her seventeenth birthday coming up in five weeks' time, except this year she wasn't having a party. She was going to do what Chelsea had decided to do for her birthday next weekend; take her two best friends somewhere special for the weekend.

Cat was going to ask Holly, Ashley's stepmother to take them and chaperone them. There was no way she wanted Winnie to accompany them.

"Cat!" Ashley snapped her fingers.

"Sorry, Ash." Cat shook her head, clearing her deep thoughts. "What did you say?"

"I think it's snack time," Ashley slapped her book closed, stood up, and stretched. "We've been studying for almost four hours now."

"Do you want to come back to Cupids Bow and go for a ride?" Cat asked her.

"I'd love to," Ashley said. "I'll call Holly and ask her if she can take us."

"Okay," Cat nodded, following Ashley out of the room and down the stairs.

They walked out of the house and walked a few blocks to Holly's bakery. The aroma that hit them when they walked into the shop made Cat's mouth water. Holly was such a good baker and cook that she swore if she had to live at the Cuthbert's she'd be as big as a house.

"How do you stay so skinny living with Holly?" Cat sighed, eyeing out all the yummy baked goods as they made their way to the counter.

Dove Bakery was always busy. Cat, Chelsea, and Ashley used to think Holly was a white witch who baked love into each one of her confectioneries. That's why her bakery always had a flow of people in and out. Once you'd had one of her loved, filled treats you wanted to come back for more warm, lovable deliciousness.

"Hi girls, how's the studying going?" Wanda, a waitress who worked for Holly, smiled at them.

"Okay, I guess," Cat told her. "What's special today?"

Cat hopped up on a stool at the counter while Ashley went through to the back to find Holly.

"Ah, we have marshmallow cheesecake." Wanda grinned. "Your favorite."

Wanda walked over to the one display cabinet and pulled out the last piece of the dessert.

"Wanda, you always know how to make a bad day so much sweeter," Cat told her with a sigh as Wanda dished the cheesecake up for her. "Do you have any of that sticky toffee sauce for the top?"

"I do." Wanda winked and brought the bowl of topping. "I also have rainbow sprinkles." She put the shaker in front of Cat. "You look like you could use a boost."

"Thank you, Wanda," Cat scooped sticky toffee sauce onto the tart and then filled it with sprinkles.

"Cat!" Holly's voice made Cat jump as she was about to take a big spoonful of dessert. "Are you eating dessert at this time of day?"

"And?" Cat shoved the spoonful of cheesecake into her mouth before Holly could take it away from her.

"Can I share?" Ashley jumped onto the stool next to Cat and picked up a spoon.

"Of course," Cat said with her hand over her mouth. "We have to eat it quickly before it gets taken away from us."

The girls giggled as they shoved spoonfuls of the tart into their mouths, guarding their plate of dessert.

"Wanda, is this your doing?" Holly laughed, watching the teenagers wolf the tart down.

"Aww, come on now, Holly." Wanda patted Holly's shoulder. "They've been studying hard the whole afternoon. I think they deserve it."

"True," Holly agreed. "I'll let you two have that today because I know how hard you are working at school."

"Thank you!" Cat and Ashley said around their mouthfuls of tart.

"Ashley tells me you want me to take you out to Cupids Bow," Holly asked them, leaning on the counter in front of them.

"If you can, please," Cat drank some of the water Wanda put in front of her and Ashley.

"Sure." Holly nodded. "As long as I get to ride as well."

"Of course," Cat said. "You're always welcome to ride along with us."

"Well, if you can keep up with us, that is." Ashley laughed at the black look Holly shot her.

"I'm not as young and supple as I once was," Holly defended her riding ability. "Besides, I don't get to ride as often as I once did."

"You ride expertly, Aunt Holly," Cat assured her. "You can ride Joker."

"Oh, great." Holly laughed. "I know the reason behind that horse's name." She reminded Cat.

"He's a sweetie," Ashley defended Joker. "Joker is just misunderstood and a bit eccentric."

"Why don't you ride him then?" Cat asked Ashley.

"Because neither your father, stable manager nor Zac will let me," Ashley reminded Cat. "Remember the last time I tried to ride Joker."

"Oh yes." Cat rolled her eyes. "My father nearly had a heart attack."

"Exactly." Ashley nodded. "So, I think it's best if none of us ride him."

"We can figure it out when we're back at the ranch," Cat told her, finishing off the dessert before wiping her mouth and getting off the stool. "Ready?"

"Would you mind closing up tonight, Wanda?" Holly asked the woman.

"No at all. You three go enjoy riding them beasts," Wanda grinned.

"You really need to try and ride again, Wanda," Ashley told her.

"I never believed that nonsense about getting back up on the horse when you've been thrown off," Wanda said. "And I ain't going to be taking any chances ever again." She laughed. "One broken leg and dislocated shoulder were more than enough for me."

"If you change your mind, let me know. I have just the horse to get you riding again," Cat assured Wanda before they said their goodbyes and headed to Cupids Bow.

They'd been riding for almost an hour when they came across Chelsea riding up from the direction of Cupids creek.

"Chelsea!" Cat called, startling her.

Chelsea reigned in Spartan and turned him towards them, "Hi Cat." She smiled.

"Been swimming in the creek?" Cat asked her.

"No, I've just been letting Spartan stretch his legs now that he's healed," Chelsea told them.

"You must be so relieved that he's recovered," Ashley said.

"I am," Chelsea patted Spartan's neck. "I don't know what I'd do without my baby."

"He's beautiful, Chelsea," Holly said.

"Yes, he is." Cat smiled at Holly.

"I'd better get back home," Chelsea told them. "I haven't finished studying for the test."

"We spent the entire afternoon studying." Cat rolled her eyes. "We missed you with us today."

"Yes, you haven't been to study with us in weeks," Ashley moaned, not letting her horse get too close to Spartan. The horses didn't like each other and the last time they got too close Spartan bit Turin, her horse.

"My mom and dad have me studying with them," Chelsea explained. "You know, as doctors, they think they're the math and science experts."

"Well, they are brilliant people," Cat confirmed. "As soon as you can come up for air, we shall all go for milkshakes at the diner."

"I can't wait." Chelsea sighed. "I'm so over all these tests."

"This is an important year, next year is our final school year." Ashley looked between Cat and Chelsea. "We have to make every test and moment count."

"You're right," Holly agreed. "You and I have to get back to Lewistown soon, Ashley."

"I'll see you both at school tomorrow," Chelsea said before riding off towards Mountain Rise.

"We'd better get back." Cat turned Zeus back towards the ranch house. "I wish I was going back to Lewistown with you."

"Oh, Kitty Cat," Ashley said. "I wish you could move in with us until you could go out on your own."

"I wish I could too," Cat admitted. "I have never been so unhappy at Cupids Bow as I have been since my dad married Winnie."

"Oh, honey," Holly's voice was filled with compassion. "I wish there was something I could do."

"Adopt me." Cat laughed. "Then I can move away from this place that was once my happy place but is now nothing more but a dark, gloomy dungeon."

"It can't be that bad," Ashley said. "Why don't I come and

stay by you tonight?" She looked at Holly. "Do you think I could?"

"Sure, you can," Holly told her. "I will tell your father when I get home. We can have a date night tonight."

"Great, it's settled then," Cat said.

"I think we should ask your father first, Cat," Holly suggested.

"No, it'll be fine," Cat assured Holly.

When they got back to the stables they were greeted by Callum. "Hello, ladies," he greeted them with a big smile and tilted his hat.

"Hello, Callum," Holly dismounted as the stable hand came to take her horse. "How are things at Cupids Ranch?"

"It's good," Callum said. "But my daughter seems to spend more time away from home these days." He stepped up to take Zeus' reins, but the horse started to fidget and pull away from him. "Whoa, boy."

"Dad, please, you need to step back," Cat hissed. "Zeus is having a problem with you."

"Maybe, Kitty Cat, his problem is with you," Callum bellowed. "He was perfect around me before you started this feud between us."

"No, dad!" Cat shouted back at him. "You're the one who started this. You're so blinded by that woman."

"Cat!" Callum bellowed again and reached up towards his daughter.

Zeus didn't like that, and he reared up at Callum. Cat was expecting it and tumbled off his back.

"Cat!" Ashley slid off her horse as Zac rode up towards the stables.

"Cat!" Zac shouted, dismounting his horse and rushing over to where Cat had fallen.

"Kitty Cat!" Callum tried to get near Cat, but Zeus wasn't having it. He reared at Callum again. His nostrils were flaring, and his head was shaking as his eyes rolled. His ears flattened.

"Dad, please go!" Cat shouted, trying to stand up.

She felt woozy and pain shot through her head. "Zeus." She soothed, grabbing his reins. "Steady boy."

Zeus snorted and pranced. Cat's soft words soothed him, but every time Callum tried to get near Cat—who was looking pale and blood was running down her forehead—he acted nervously.

"Zac, calm Zeus down, I need to get to Cat," Callum said.

"Dad, get away!" Cat said again.

"Dad, listen to Cat, you are stirring the horse up again, you know how protective he is over Cat," Zac pointed out.

"Callum," Holly stood next to him. "Let's take a few steps back."

"Cat is hurt," Callum's voice was filled with worry. "That beast hurt her."

"No, Callum, you didn't listen to Cat," Holly pointed out. "I believe it was you that upset the horse."

"I think my husband is correct," Winnie's voice made everyone turn towards her. "That beast rolls his eyes every time I get close to him. Maybe it's time to get rid of him."

"You leave my horse alone," Cat's head popped around an agitated Zeus. "Please step back so I can calm him down."

"I think we need to give Cat and Zeus their space," Ashley intervened. "Uncle Callum, is it okay for me to stay tonight?"

"Of course, my dear, you know you're always welcome here," Callum gave her a warm smile.

"But Callum, we have not prepared for a guest tonight," Winnie said disapprovingly.

"Cat's friends are always welcome here whenever they want." Callum's voice was firm and brooked no argument. "They are family, not guests."

Winnie looked taken aback by it like she'd struck him. "So be it then."

Winnie turned and stalked off. That's when Cat saw it in her father's eyes. A flash of anger and disdain she'd never seen before. There was definitely a rift in the relationship. Cat was sure of it. Once Zeus settled down Cat walked him to the stables while Ashley said goodbye to Holly and ran after her

"Cat, are you okay?" Ashley asked her, walking into the stables where Cat now had Zeus and was taking off his saddle.

"I'm fine," Cat lied. "Just got a little bit of a headache." She was feeling really woozy.

But Cat had to push through it because Zeus wouldn't calm down if he felt her pain.

"Winnie wouldn't really try and get rid of Zeus, would she?" Ashley reached up and rubbed the big black thoroughbred's forehead.

"She'd do anything to try and torture me," Cat said softly. "Hey, boy, I'm so sorry you had to deal with all that." She cooed softly to the horse.

"No wonder Zeus dislikes her," Ashley said. "Why is he being so antsy around your father though?"

"My father and I had a huge fight in the stables a few days ago," Cat explained. "He told me that I needed to train Zeus not to bite. But he never bites."

"I know, Zeus didn't even bite Spartan back that time he was bitten," Ashley said, rubbing the horse's ears. "I've never seen him bite anyone." She frowned. "Okay, he did bite that one stable hand once."

"Yes, but for good reason," Cat pointed out, picking up Zeus's brush and starting to brush him down. "The man was whipping the horses."

"True, Zeus is quite the hero," Ashley smiled. "The only other time I've seen Zeus get aggressive was when Turin got bitten by Spartan that time."

"Oh, yes!" Cat's eyes widened. "He ran at Spartan and there was nearly a full blow horse fight."

"Zac popped up from nowhere and stopped the horses," Ashley shook her head. "He was so crazy to run in between them like that. Zeus and Spartan aren't exactly small horses. They are both very powerful horses."

"Pure Turin," Cat shook her head. "I can't believe that Spartan would take a bite out of him like that."

"Spartan can be quite the bully when he wants to be," Ashley said. "That bite nearly got infected. Thank goodness for Dr. Solly, that new vet in town."

"You mean the young hunky new vet in town." Cat laughed. "Chelsea and I have seen the way you ogle him out all coy and blushing."

"No!" Ashley's face once again turned bright red. "It's not like that. I just think he's so nice, sweet, and funny."

"He is also about eight or nine years older than us," Cat pointed out and shuddered. "Way too old for you."

"I wasn't looking at him like that," Ashley said defensively. "Although if I was older maybe!"

"Ah, ha," Cat said. "I knew you had a crush on him."

"At least it's a crush on a person who's here in flesh and blood." Ashley picked up another brush and started brushing Zeus on the opposite side. "He really loves the attention, doesn't he?" She laughed when Zeus nuzzled her hair in appreciation of her brushing him.

"He's just trying to say thank you and show you that he loves you." Cat laughed.

"Aww," Ashley rubbed Zeus's forehead and kissed him. "I love you, big boy. But don't let Turin know because he thinks he's the only horse I love."

"I love Turin's liver-chestnut color," Cat said, as the stable hand brought a cooled down and groomed Turin back into the stable to put him in the stall next to his friend, Zeus."

"Yes, that dark brown mane and tail really make him stand out," Ashley agreed. "So does the scar from Spartan's bite."

"It makes him that more attractive to the mares." Cat laughed.

"But Spartan is the true beauty in this stable," Ashley brushed along his side to hindquarters. "He is pure black and his coat shines like silk."

"That's very poetic of you," Cat told her, turning when the stable hand came to help them.

"I can take over now." The young man smiled at Cat and

Ashley. "Turin is all settled for the evening. I'll just tend to Zeus and Joker before feeding them."

"Thank you so much, Tommy," Cat and Ashley said together before saying goodbye to Zeus and Turin and then heading back to the house.

"Now we have to go and face the wicked witch of Cupids Bow Ranch." Ashley linked her arm through Cat's, and they walked into the house through the kitchen door together.

"Cat!" Bessie's eyes widened when she saw the congealed blood on Cat's forehead. "Goodness, child." She immediately ran to the one cabinet and pulled out a first aid kit. "Come sit down so I can tend to that nasty gash."

"I'm fine, Bessie." Cat tried to reassure her.

"No, Bessie, she is not." Ashley pushed Cat towards a kitchen chair and made her sit down. "I know you were lying to me at the stable about feeling okay."

"Fine, I have a bit of a headache," Cat admitted while sitting down. She knew she wasn't going to win when Bessie and Ashley had ganged up on her. "It's just a scratch on my head. I told my father to back off, but as with everything else lately, he didn't listen."

"That, young lady, is no scratch." Bessie put disinfectant on the wound to clean it, making Cat flinch with the sting of the substance. "Sorry, love, but I have to clean it out."

"Cat, we should take you to the doctor," Ashley's eyes widened once she saw the gash after it had been cleaned.

"No, not doctors," Cat said before looking at Bessie curiously, "Is everything okay between my father and his new wife?" Cat asked Bessie as she put a band-aid on the cut.

"Why do you ask?" Bessie's eyes narrowed when she looked at Cat.

"Because I saw dad be a little abrupt with her, and he's never like that unless someone has really angered him," Cat explained.

"I'm not sure but I have heard a lot of arguing this past month." Bessie packed up the first aid kit.

"Seems like after not even a full year the honeymoon is finally over!" Ashley pulled a face.

"We can only hope," Cat said. She knew it was spiteful and immensely selfish of her to say something so hateful. But Winnie did nothing but make Cat's life as hellish as possible.

Chapter Six

REASONS - PART THREE

PRESENT DAY

"I remember when Winnie tried to get rid of Zeus," Zac said. "I'm so sorry you had such a bad time with Winnie. I wish I'd listened better."

"You were all giddy in love with Chelsea at the time," Cat said with a shrug. "I guess both you and daddy were just preoccupied."

There was a knock on the door. Cat and Zac exchanged a quizzical glance.

"Are you expecting anyone?" Zac asked Cat.

"No," Cat said, shaking her head. "No one knows about my house. Except for Maria and West."

"Is West coming here?" Zac asked her.

"Yes, why?" Cat frowned.

"I often wondered if the two of you would end up together," Zac admitted to her.

"Uh... no." Cat shook her head. "West and I are nothing more than good friends and then there's the complication of him being my manager."

"That hasn't stopped a lot of other people from having a relationship," Zac pointed out.

The knock came again. "I'd better get the door."

Cat walked to the front door and pulled it open. She was shocked to find Chelsea standing there.

"Hi," Chelsea said, looking a little nervous. "I'm sorry to barge in. I was looking for Zac and Janine told me he was here with you."

"Hi," Cat greeted Chelsea. "Yes, he is." She stepped back so Chelsea could enter. "Zac is in the lounge."

"Thank you," Chelsea said, stepping around her. "How are you?"

"I'm good." Cat gave her a smile. "How are you feeling?"

"Mostly numb," Chelsea told her. "When my dad died, I can remember feeling this crushing weight in my chest and a squeezing pressure around my heart."

"I can relate to that feeling," Cat said softly, rubbing her arm comfortingly. "I'm so sorry about your mom. I haven't been able to say that to you in the past few days."

"You were such a great help," Chelsea told her. "I don't know what I would've done if you and David hadn't shown up that day." Tears misted Chelsea's eyes.

"I'm glad we could be there for you." Cat walked with her to the lounge. "Zac, Chelsea came to see you."

"Chelsea?" Zac raised his eyebrows. "Hi!" He tried to push himself awkwardly to his feet.

"Don't get up," Chelsea said to him and sat down on the sofa.

"Can I get you some coffee or other refreshment?" Cat asked her.

"Just a bottle of water, please," Chelsea told her.

"Sure," Cat went to the kitchen to get the water, wondering what Chelsea wanted with Zac or why she was here.

When Cat walked into the lounge and gave Chelsea the water, she heard Zac tell her that Cat was telling him the story about why she left home all those years ago. Cat watched

Chelsea's eyes widen and look at her in panic. Cat knew why she was looking at her like that too.

"Are you okay, Chelsea?" Zac asked.

"Uh...yes. Why?" Chelsea looked at Zac.

"You've gone pale," Zac told her.

"No, I'm good," Chelsea told him. "I just got frightened when Cat walked into the room. I've been jumpy since my mom died."

"I can understand that." Zac smiled. "Are you going to continue your story?" He looked at Cat.

"I don't think Chelsea's interested in my story," Cat said. "She came here to see you."

"I've always wondered what made you leave Montana," Chelsea looked at Cat.

"Zac and I can finish this another day," Cat told them, feeling uncomfortable about continuing her story in front of Chelsea.

"No, I'm here today so I need to know," Zac told her.

"I'm not comfortable doing this now, Zac." Cat looked at Chelsea. "What are you doing here?"

"I have something to discuss with Zac about Mountain Rise," Chelsea told them.

"I'll go and leave you two to talk," Cat was about to leave, but Zac stopped her. "Come on Cat, I need to know the end of your story."

"It's nearly finished," Cat told him. "I can continue this tomorrow."

"No, it's okay, I'll go and come back later," Chelsea started to get up.

"It's okay," Cat stopped Chelsea from going. "I'll finish my story."

"Cat, you have to invite Chelsea with us for your birthday weekend," Ashley told Cat.

"Ashley, Chelsea lied to us for six months about dating Zac," Cat reminded her. "She made it quite clear where her loyalties lie."

"I know." Ashley shook her head, sadness reflecting in her eyes. "But it's just not the same without her. It's been four weeks since we found out she and Zac were dating. Maybe it's time to forgive them both?"

"Not a chance," Cat said stubbornly. "Besides, I'm not angry with either of them for dating. You can't help who you fall in love with. We think our lives are in our control but they're really not. We don't decide who our hormones respond to."

"Are you trying to analyze love?" Ashley looked at Cat in amazement.

"Why do you look so surprised?" Cat frowned at Ashley. "I can analyze things."

"I know." Ashley tilted her looking at Cat with narrowed eyes. "Is there something else going on between you, Chelsea, and Zac that I don't know about?"

"Not with Chelsea, I just don't trust her anymore," Cat closed her school locker after getting the books for her next class. "As for Zac, he keeps taking Winnie the witch's side over mine."

"I noticed that when I stayed over on the weekend," Ashley told Cat.

"I'm so glad you've been staying over these past three weekends since Chelsea's seventeenth birthday." Cat looked at her wristwatch. "I don't know what I would've done at home without you."

"It's a pleasure," Ashley assured her. "Besides, I get to spend time with you and ride Turin more often."

"Can Holly still take us to Billings for my birthday next

weekend?" Cat asked as she and Ashley started to walk towards their next class.

"Yes," Ashley nodded. "You know it's not going to be the same without Chelsea."

"I know," Cat stopped at the door to the room. "And you're right, I will find Chelsea during lunch break and talk to her."

"See, you can be forgiving." Ashley smiled happily and pushed the door open.

They walked into class and took their seats. Cat spent most of the English lesson thinking about what she was going to say to Chelsea. She knew she'd been harsh on Chelsea. But Cat had not only been hurt about her lying about dating Cat's brother but also about how Harris felt about Chelsea. Then there was the fact that Chelsea had gone on a date with Harris behind Cat and Zac's back. Cat wondered if Chelsea had told Zac about that date.

It felt like English class had taken a lot longer than an hour. When the class was over it was break time. Ashley had band practice, so Cat was going to find Chelsea who had taken to sitting on the bleachers for lunch since their friendship had ended. Cat put her books back in her locker before going off to the fields to find Chelsea. She looked over the bleachers, but Chelsea wasn't there. Cat walked behind them, thinking maybe she was sitting in the shade reading. Chelsea loved reading and would find any excuse to hide away with a book.

Cat hadn't walked too far when she heard Chelsea laugh and that's when she found her. Only Chelsea wasn't alone. She was sitting on a picnic blanket with Harris Conway who had his arm possessively around Chelsea's shoulders.

"Still cheating on my brother, I see," Cat's icy voice had Chelsea's head spinning around and her eyes opening wide.

Chelsea sprung up from the ground in one swift move, "Cat!"

"No, no," Cat said, holding up a hand. "Don't get up or let me interrupt whatever this is."

"It's not what it looks like," Chelsea said, but her eyes and flushed cheeks told Cat it was exactly what it looked like.

"Of course, it isn't," Cat folded her arms across her chest and glared at Chelsea. "To think I came looking for you to talk and forgive you. I was going to invite you to my birthday weekend because Ashley and I actually miss you."

"Cat, please, just listen to me." Chelsea stepped off the blanket and walked closer to Cat.

"Chelsea, you don't have to explain anything," Harris said, standing up, and walking towards them.

"Please, Harris, just go!" Chelsea turned and looked at him.

"I don't think so," Harris said, his eyes narrowing on Cat. "You look like you could use some support."

"I'd listen to her if I was you, Harris," Cat jeered at him. "This is none of your business."

"Chelsea is my friend and so I'm making it my business," Harris told Cat.

"Fine," Cat said. "I'll leave you and Chelsea to your business then." She started to leave, stopped, and turned back towards them. "I can't wait to see how you explain this one to Zac." She looked at Chelsea with a smug smile. "You have told my brother about your *friendship* with Harris, right?"

"Cat..." Chelsea took another step closer to her. "Please, don't mention this to Zac. It really isn't what you think."

"If it's not what I think, why shouldn't I mean it to Zac?" Cat asked her, raising her eyebrows.

"You know, you're just jealous that for once someone finds Chelsea more appealing than you and your pretty face," Harris sneered at Cat.

"Excuse me?" Cat looked at Harris, shocked at the venom in his voice.

"You heard me," Harris told her, looking her over with disgust in his eyes. "The moment someone like me preferred the company of your best friend over you, you turned your back on her."

"Harris..." Chelsea whirled and stared at him in shocked amazement. "That's not a nice thing to say."

"See, you're doing it again," Harris pointed out to Chelsea.

"Every time I say anything about your two friends, you're so quick to jump to their defense. Yet they both turned their backs on you the minute Cat Sparrow couldn't get her way."

"You know nothing about me and Ashley," Cat's anger bubbled up hot and spilled over in a red blaze. "Me not speaking to Chelsea had nothing to do with you. You're nobody in our lives." She knew that was a nasty thing to say but Harris had insulted both Chelsea and Ashley. He was also trying to steal Zac's girlfriend.

"Cat, just leave him," Chelsea said, glaring at Harris. "You want to know why I always stand up for my friends. Because our rift was my fault. I brought it on myself."

"Why are you blaming yourself?" Harris looked at her, amazed. "If Cat and Ashley were truly your friends, they wouldn't have cut you off because you were dating Cat's brother."

"That's not why they cut me off." Chelsea's voice was laced with anger.

Cat looked at Chelsea in surprise. It took a lot to make Chelsea angry and her eyes were blazing with anger right now. That's when Cat realized that maybe she had misjudged the scene she'd witnessed. When Cat thought about it, Chelsea was leaning away from Harris like he'd hugged her to congratulate or comfort not out of affection. If Chelsea was just friends with Harris, there was nothing really to tell Zac about. She had a right to her friends just like Zac's one best friend was Gwen Ryan. Zac and Gwen had been close since they were kids. He often hugged her too.

Cat was starting to feel awful for jumping to conclusions. She was still a bit raw about Chelsea's secret date with Harris. Not because she was jealous or begrudged Chelsea's happiness but because Chelsea had withheld the information from her. They'd been friends their whole lives and had told each other everything. Good or bad. Cat suddenly realized the real reason she'd been so angry with Chelsea. It wasn't because Chelsea was dating her brother or went on a date with Harris. It was because she hadn't trusted Cat or Ashley enough to tell them the truth.

"I'm going!" Harris held up his hands in exasperation.

"That's wise," Cat told him.

Harris looked at Cat angrily, "This is the reason I don't go for girls that look like you." He said nastily. "Under all that pretty is a nasty shrew who loves to lead her pack around like an entitled spoiled queen."

"That's not what Cat is like at all!" Chelsea's voice shook with anger. "You've not heard one word I've told you."

"Quite frankly, I shut off when you started jabbering about Cat and Ashley," Harris admitted. "I thought you were different, but you were already far too indoctrinated into the Cat club to see how she is using you."

"I'd leave now if I was you!" Chelsea seethed. "For the record, I thought you were different too. I thought you were my friend."

"I tried to be," Harris told her. "I tried to pull you out of Cat Sparrow's clutches. She's just like her mother was."

"You know nothing about my mother!" Cat's voice tore out of her chest, and she was about to slap his arrogant face, but Chelsea held her back.

"He's not worth it, Cat," Chelsea told her. "How dare you say something so nasty about a woman you didn't even know?"

"Oh, I heard all about Cat's mother when we moved here," Harris's lip curled nastily. "She too had her troop of doting friends and didn't care who she trampled over."

"Leave, now!" Chelsea breathed. "I don't know where you got your poisonous information from but whoever it was, they're the bitter, twisted, poisonous ones."

"Don't you dare speak about my..." Harris's eyes blazed.

"Is everything alright here?" One of the teachers stepped toward them. "I heard angry voices."

"We're fine, thank you, Mr. Hornsby," Chelsea said through gritted teeth. "Harris was just leaving."

"I'll walk with you," Mr. Hornsby's shrewd eyes told Cat that he'd heard more than he'd let on. "Come on Harris." He pulled the young man with him. "Enjoy the rest of your lunch break, young ladies."

"Cat, I'm so sorry about everything!" Chelsea said as soon as Mr. Hornsby and Harris disappeared.

"No, Chelsea, I owe you an apology," Cat said. "I jumped to conclusions."

"It was my fault," Chelsea admitted. "I let my stupid ego get in my way. I should never have gone on that date with Harris. I knew it was wrong, but I still went."

"I should've let you explain when I'd gotten over my shock after finding out about you, Zac, and Harris," Cat told her.

The two of them hugged.

"Were you coming to find me?" Chelsea asked as Cat helped her pack up her blanket.

"I was coming to talk things out and invite you to my birthday weekend." Cat picked up Chelsea's book. "I see you got the book I left for you?"

"I did slip a note into your locker thanking you for it," Chelsea told her.

"I didn't find that," Cat told her. "But then again my locker is kind of full of stuff."

"That's because I haven't been there to organize it for you." Chelsea laughed. "I bet Ashley's Locker is in even worse shape than yours."

"It really is," Cat said and laughed. "Who do you think told Harris all those terrible things about my mother?"

"I don't know." Chelsea shook her head. "Maybe his mother?"

"I thought they'd only moved to Lewistown about seven months ago?" Cat looked at Ashley.

"They did," Chelsea confirmed. "He didn't speak much about his family."

"Well, let's not let him worry us," Cat told her.

"No, it was nice to see his true colors though." Chelsea took her book and blanket from Cat as they made their way back to the main school building.

"Yup," Cat agreed. "Let's find Ashley."

Chelsea stopped by her locked door which was next to Cat's to put her blanket and book away. When she opened it, a note fell out!

I really thought you were different, but you're just like all the rest of the blind squad.

"You should report him," Cat warned Chelsea. "He seems like a creep."

Chelsea shuddered. "He really does, doesn't he?"

The girls walked off towards the music hall where Ashley had band practice.

PRESENT DAY

Zac sat staring at Cat. He knew it was a long time ago, but he still felt like someone had punched him in the heart. Cat had already told Zac that she and Chelsea had known Harris from school long before he came to work as the foreman for Cupids Bow Ranch. But Cat hadn't told him that Chelsea had a date and friendship with the man back in high school at the time he and Chelsea were dating. He looked at Chelsea who sat next to him on the sofa biting her thumbnail as she always did when concentrating or was nervous.

"Chelsea, is this true?" Zac knew it was a stupid question. His sister had no reason to lie to him. Although he knew she sugar-coated her story for his benefit.

"Zac, it was a long time ago," Chelsea pointed out. "I never told you about Harris because it was nothing more than a friendship."

"You went out on a date with him when we'd been seeing each other for only five months!" Zac couldn't stop the harshness in his voice.

"Can we talk about this later?" Chelsea looked at him pleadingly. "Let Cat finish her story and then I promise to tell you mine."

"I'd love to hear that myself," Cat told them.

"Okay," Chelsea promised. "Once you've come clean I will too." She challenged Cat.

"Deal!" Cat was never one to pass up a challenge or a dare.

"Before you continue, I have a few questions," Zac said. "Why didn't either of you tell me you'd made up?"

"I thought you knew," Chelsea told him. "I mean, I went to Billings for the weekend with Cat, Holly, and Ashley for Cat's seventeenth birthday."

"Chelsea was also at my eighteenth birthday, and she spent many nights in between that at the ranch," Cat pointed out. "I also spent a *lot* of time at the Hitchins farm to get away from Winniezilla."

"I forgot Ashley came up with that name for your stepmom." Chelsea and Cat looked at each other and burst out laughing at their inside joke.

Zac watched the two of them laugh and exchange some banter on why Ashley had named Winnie that. He may be hurt and angry at Chelsea right now for her betrayal, which was crazy he knew, all those years ago. But it was so good to see her really laugh again.

"Okay, I get it, you had a lot of nicknames for Winnie," Zac interrupted Cat and Chelsea's trip down memory lane. "I can't believe I didn't know you two had become friends again."

"You went back to finish your degree once you were well enough to," Cat explained. "So, you weren't there for most of the year between my seventeenth and eighteenth birthday."

"Then that means you two had another falling out after Cat's eighteenth birthday," Zac realized.

"Something like that!" Cat said and Zac noticed both hers and Chelsea's shoulders stiffen. They also exchanged a look that he couldn't quite decipher.

"Oh, you two both have some serious explaining to do here!" Zac looked from Cat to Chelsea. "In fact, no one leaves this house until we have all this dirty laundry nice and freshly cleaned."

"I think that's an excellent idea," Cat said, looking at Chelsea with narrowed eyes.

"I agree," Chelsea nodded.

"Good," Zac said, sitting back against the cushions once again. "Cat, please continue your story."

He watched both women closely. Zac knew by the look they'd exchanged that whatever the second blow-up between them was, it was a lot more than Chelsea having a date with Harris Conway. That look was filled with fear, uncertainty, and a dash of angry mistrust. Now, when he looked back to when he'd come home after being told the news about his father, it wasn't just Cat giving Chelsea the cold shoulder. Chelsea had been scared of Cat.

Why on earth would Chelsea be scared of Cat? He frowned and watched Cat pour them each another cup of coffee from the pot. *Back then Cat had been cold to Chelsea. She'd completely ignored her like she wasn't there.*

Zac braced himself as Cat sat back cradling her coffee mug because he had a feeling what Cat was about to tell him was a lot more chilling. He understood why Cat had told what she had. She was pointing out the most significant examples of how Winnie had emotionally tortured Cat. But she'd also been building the scene for the final showdown when everything came to a head and Cat had left home for good.

THIRTY-TWO YEARS AGO - CAT'S STORY CONTINUED

Cat stretched in her nice, warm bed and lay back smiling up at the ceiling. Today was going to be a good day. As much as she may try, her step monster Winnie was not going to ruin Cat's eighteenth birthday the way she'd tried to ruin her last two. Cat couldn't believe the horrible woman had tried to wheedle her way into coming for the traditional father-daughter birthday dinner that night. But for the first time in three years, her father had put his foot down and told Winnie there was no way she was coming with. Callum had even thrown Cat's mother in her face telling Winnie. He'd told Winnie that not even Grace had been invited to the dinner Callum took Zac and Cat to on their birthdays.

Winnie had been so angry she'd snuck into Cat's room late the previous night to let her know that Cat mustn't get too big-headed about her not coming with them. That she'd find a way to get Callum to let her join them before warning Cat not to tell her father any more lies about her. Except they weren't lies! If anyone told lies in this house, it was Winnie. Even Bessie knew that and there had been many times Winnie had tried to get Bessie fired. The woman just didn't seem to understand that everyone who lived and worked on the ranch was family to Callum. And family meant everything to Cat's father. Cat shook thoughts of Winnie from her head. Even just thinking about the woman was letting her win and today the only winner was going to be Cat. She was turning eighteen today.

Zac would be home for her birthday later that day. Ashley and Chelsea were coming over for a special lunch Bessie was preparing for her and her friends. She didn't want a big party, but her father had insisted, and they were going to do something on Saturday at the ranch. He'd invited some of the other four ranches that surrounded to a barn dance at Cupids Bow in the old cow barn. Ashley and Chelsea had invited some kids from their school. It was going to be fun. Chelsea only hoped that Winnie the witch wasn't going to do her usual thing and try to make everything about her.

"Good grief, Cat," Cat admonished herself, flinging her legs over the side of her bed to get up. "You can't go a few minutes without the witch creeping into your thoughts. It's what she wants, so stop it!"

Cat took a deep breath and cleared her mind before turning to the picture of her mom that sat on her nightstand. The glass was cracked but Cat wasn't going to reflect on how that had happened, because it would once again bring that witch into her thoughts.

"I wish you were here, momma," Cat said to her mother's picture. "I think I would be looking forward to the dance tomorrow a whole lot more if you were." She picked the picture up. "I think the reason I have enjoyed my birthdays since my thirteenth as much is that a part of me was always missing without you here."

"Come now, sweetheart," Cat could hear her mother say. *"You know I am always with you. You and your brother are each part of my heart which beats inside of yours."* Cat put her hand on her heart pretending it was her mother's. *"Every beat of your heart is a beat of mine no matter where I am, as long as your heart beats, I'm with you."*

Cat sighed and put the picture back on her nightstand. Her father kept telling her he'd replace the picture frame, but she wouldn't let him. The frame had belonged to her mother and each part of it was precious to Cat. Even broken, it still held all its memories in it, even those tainted by Winnie's jealous rage that had broken it.

"I love you, momma," Cat said softly, kissing her fingertips and touching them in the picture.

Cat got up and went to have a shower. Although it was Friday, there was no school today. It was a day off due to some emergency teacher conference which couldn't have happened on a better day as far as Cat and her friends were concerned. Ashley and Chelsea were arriving soon. They were all going riding before their lunch, and then Holly was coming to fetch them to take them to the Lewistown fair that was currently on. Cat was going to have a shower and change at Ashley's house before her father fetched her for their dinner.

Chapter Seven

REASONS - PART FOUR

THIRTY-TWO YEARS AGO - CAT'S STORY CONTINUED

It had been a great day so far and was looking even better when Cat's father fetched her from the Cuthbert's house for her birthday dinner without Winnie in tow.

"Hi, daddy," Cat greeted Callum, climbing into the passenger seat of the pickup truck.

"Hi, honey, how was your day so far?" Callum waited until Cat was buckled in before waving goodbye to the Cuthberts and taking off to drive to the fanciest restaurant in town.

"It was awesome, thank you," Cat told him excitedly. "Holly, Ashley, and Chelsea helped me choose an awesome outfit for my dance tomorrow night."

"That's great, honey." Callum gave her a smile.

"What's wrong?" Cat's eyes narrowed. "Please don't tell me that Winnie is waiting for us at the restaurant. Because if she is, you can turn the truck around and drop me back at Ashley's."

"No, Winnie is not with us tonight," Callum promised. "But, honey, I really wish you'd try harder with her. You didn't even think to invite her on your girls' day today nor did you include her in decorating the barn for your dance."

"I'm not going to argue with you tonight, or the rest of the weekend, dad," Cat told him. "Because it's my eighteenth birthday weekend. So, this weekend is NOT about Winnie, it's about me for a change." Her eyes narrowed a little more. "I don't like her. I've never said otherwise. I don't trust her and there are things about her you don't know. You have blinders on when it comes to her and no matter what horrible things she does to me I'm always somehow to blame."

"Kitty Cat..." Callum looked at her in surprise.

"No," Cat butted in to what he was about to say. "It's my day to remember, so only I get to speak right now, and then I don't want to mention your wife again. Because I don't want her ruining yet another birthday for me."

"Fine!" Callum relented. "But we are going to have a conversation about this young lady."

"No, daddy, we are not," Cat told him. "You never listen, you only speak over me, and besides, I'm not here in Lewistown for much longer."

"What do you mean by that?" Callum looked at her in shock as he parked the car in the restaurant parking lot.

"Daddy, we've spoken about this for years," Cat threw up her hand in exasperation. "I'm moving to Nashville to go and live with Aunty Simone in a few months after I graduate high school."

"I thought that was just one of your options?" Callum stared at her wide-eyed.

"No, daddy, it's been my plan since I was about ten," Cat reminded him. "My plan has never changed."

"We can discuss this closer to the time," Callum told her, unfastening his seatbelt. "Let's go and enjoy your birthday dinner because I have something for you and something to tell you too."

"Uh-oh!" Cat unbuckled her seatbelt and slid out of the truck. "Are you seeing someone else, getting a divorce, or something?"

"What?" Callum frowned as they walked into the restaurant. "Why on earth would you say something like that?"

"Because that's the exact thing you said to Zac and me before dropping the Winnie bomb on us," Cat pointed out.

"Good evening, birthday girl," the restaurant's owner greeted them. "Happy birthday!"

He leaned over and kissed Cat on the cheek.

"Thank you," Cat gave the man who'd known her since before she could walk a big smile.

"I have your special dessert for you tonight," he told Cat and winked. "Because it's your eighteenth, I made extra for you to take home with you."

"No way!" Cat's eyes lit up. "You are the best." She gave him a big hug before following him to their usual table.

"A waiter will be with you shortly," he told them with a big smile then walked off saying. "Enjoy your evening."

Cat had been so excited when they'd walked into the restaurant, that she hadn't even noticed the box in her father's hand. It was the size of a flat jewelry box. It was carved with their surname on the top with two horses rearing up at each with Cupid standing beneath them, aiming his bow. Just like the logo on the gate of Cupids Bow Ranch.

"Wow, daddy, that's a beautiful carving on that box," Cat noted. "It looks just like the Ranch's logo."

"Yes, it is a family heirloom," Callum told her. "Now that you're eighteen, it is my honor to pass it on to you."

Cat's eyes widened, "Really?" She looked at the box excitedly. "Can I see it?"

"Yes," Callum put his hand on it before Cat could pull it away from him. "But first, we need to talk."

Cat slouched back in her chair, rolled her eyes, and sighed, "Daddy, please can we not talk about Winnie tonight." She closed her eyes to quelch her anger. "For just one birthday. I want to enjoy one birthday without her besmirching it."

"This is not about Winnie," Callum surprised her by saying.

"It's about your legacy, Cupids Bow Ranch, and the land we look after."

"Well, that I can listen to," Cat leaned forward on the table.

Cat's father told her the story of how the Sparrows came to get the land they live on now. More importantly, he explained what the Sparrows' promise was to the previous guardians of the land. Cat had been enthralled by the tale and even promised to keep the details to herself unless a time came when she needed to use the information to save the land. She'd felt so important to be the keeper of the Cupids Bow legacy. Cat felt doubly important when Callum had given her the ancient box. A box that she learned was carved by one of the previous guardians of the land, especially for the first Sparrow to live in Lewistown.

Call pulled the small key out and handed it to her. "You must guard the treasures in this box at all times, Kitty Cat. Remember your promise. No one other than you has laid eyes on this box since my daddy gave it to me on my eighteenth birthday."

"Don't worry, Daddy," Cat promised. "I will keep it safe and not let another set of eyes look upon it until I'm ready to hand it to the next Sparrow."

"That's my girl," Callum said proudly.

Cat opened the box in which was an ancient leather-bound journal. The name Adrian Sparrow was engraved on the cover.

"Is this the journal of the first Sparrow to live on Cupids Bow?" Cat looked up at Callum in awe.

"It is," Callum confirmed. "Now it is yours to read and learn from."

Cat put the white gloves on the side of the box and gently opened the book.

"It's in French." She looked up at Callum.

"Now you know why I insisted you learn the language," Callum told her with a laugh.

"Yes, it does make sense now," Cat said. "Thank you, Daddy, this is awesome."

Cat pulled the gloves off, put them back where they belonged, closed and locked the box.

"But that's not your only present, honey," Cat pulled another brightly wrapped box from his pocket. "This is the other part." He put it on the table and slid it over to her.

Cat's eyes lit up as she pulled off the wrapper and found a jewelry box inside. She opened it, and tears immediately misted her eyes when she saw her mother's ruby necklace in it.

"This is yours now too, Kitty Cat," Callum said softly. "Along with your mother's charm bracelet." He pulled yet another box from his pocket and gave it to her.

"Dad, thank you," Cat stood up and gave him a big hug across the table. Not caring that tears were now sliding down her cheeks.

It had been such a shock to see her mother's ruby necklace, which was also a family heirloom like the charm bracelet. Cat picked the necklace on and slipped it over her neck. The chain was long enough, so she did not have to undo the clasp. It could also be hidden beneath her shirt to keep close to her heart. Callum helped her put the bracelet on.

"I know these will bring you a lot of luck and prosperity, my angel," Callum stood up, leaned over the table, and kissed her on the head. "Your mother would be so proud of the beautiful woman you're becoming."

"Thank you, daddy," Cat said through her tears, wiping at her cheeks. "You have no idea how much I wish she was here right now."

"Me too, angel. Me too," Callum's eyes were also misted with tears. "Ah, here comes the food. Just in time, because I'm starving."

"Me too," Cat said, her mouth-watering as her food was put in front of her.

Cat was still a little angry with Chelsea. She couldn't believe after everything Harris had put them through the day they'd become friends again. She still even spoke to the guy. But once again Chelsea had kept secrets from her, and Cat had caught them down by Cupids Creek. Harris even had the nerve to ask Cat if she was stalking him and Chelsea on her own land! Cupids Bow Ranch's neighbors were lucky that Callum allowed them to use the creek as a picnic, fishing, and swimming spot at all. As the name implied, it belonged to Cupids Bow and not the Hitchins.

"Honey, are you going to be angry about whatever's going on in your head the whole day?" Callum asked her.

"Sorry, no, daddy," Cat said and shook her head. "I'm just thinking that maybe it's time to close off Cupids creek from the rest of our neighbors."

"Why would you want to do that?" Callum asked her. "Do you think the sign would look better on the far wall?"

Cat and Callum were getting the Cupids Bow indoor arena ready for the annual Cupids Bow Horse show.

"Yes, definitely on that wall," Cat agreed with her father. "Whenever you've put it on the other wall, people have hardly seen it."

"That's exactly what your brother said," Callum told her. He was on the back of his horse King Callum fondly known as King. "Do you want me to ask one of the stable hands to get it from the storage shed?" Cat asked him.

"If you could, honey, that would be great." Callum turned to look at her. "While you're gone, I'm going to take King around the ring once more to ensure there are no more holes."

"Okay, daddy, I'll get Bessie to bring some of her homemade lemonade as well," Cat told him.

She turned to go when there was a crash from one of the viewing boxes. Cat and Callum's eyes met as they looked at each other in fright. Her first thought was that it was Winnie spying on them, which made her heart drop. Callum and Cat had checked the stables and the arena before they began working. They'd meet once a week for Cat to go over what she was reading in Adrian Sparrow's journal, and they did not want others to know.

"I'll go see who it is, daddy." Cat turned and dashed up the stairs before Callum could stop her.

"No, Cat, wait," Callum called after her.

As Cat got to the top of the stairs, a familiar figure pushed past her. She didn't get a good view of who it was because he had a hoodie pulled low over his face. But even with that on she could guess who it was by their build and height. Without thinking, Cat gave chase but before she could get out of the door, she was stopped by Chelsea.

"Cat!" Chelsea breathed. "Stop!"

"What are you doing here?" Cat hissed at her. "Why are you getting in my way of chasing down the intruder?"

Anger bubbled up in Cat.

"Please, Cat, let him go, he means no harm," Chelsea pleaded. "He just needed a place to stay for a few nights and he could stay in my barn."

"So, you put your side fling in my barn?" Cat was even more outraged with Chelsea.

"What?" Chelsea's brows knit together as she looked at Cat confused. "He's not my fling."

"Whatever, Chelsea, you'd better find him and tell him to get his stuff out of the stables before tonight." Cat seethed. "The show starts tomorrow, and we don't house vagrants."

"Cat, please listen to me, you don't understand!" Chelsea tried to plead with her again.

"Just leave, Chelsea," Cat told her. "And don't show your face near me again. Because now I have to lie to my brother once again."

"Why do you have to lie to your brother?" Chelsea looked even more confused. "He knows about this."

"Zac knows?" Cat almost choked. "And he's okay with you putting another guy up in our stables?"

"I don't know what you're talking about," Chelsea looked at Cat.

"Just go," Cat told her rudely.

"I need to get his things," Chelsea said nervously wringing her hands.

"You can come back later when the stables are clear," Cat told her, blocking the door. "Now, please leave, or I'll have you escorted off my land."

Chelsea's eyes misted over with tears, but she said no more, just turned, got back on Spartan, and took off towards her ranch.

Cat stood staring after her, her chest heaving in anger. She went back to where her father was trotting King around the arena.

"Is everything okay?" Callum must've seen how angry Cat was.

"Thanks for the backup," Cat said to him.

"I saw it was Chelsea and figured you were in no danger," Callum told her.

"That's what you think!" Cat said beneath her breath. Now she had to hunt the last person she ever wanted to speak to again and find out how much of their conversation he'd heard. Or rather if he could speak French because they only spoke about the journal and her the Cupids Bow legacy in French. "I'm going to get the ladder."

"Hold up, young lady," Callum galloped over to her.

Before Cat knew what was happening, he scooped her up off her feet and plopped her down in front of him. Like he'd done so many times when she was a child. Cat giggled as Callum galloped them around the arena.

"You're crazy, daddy. You're going to throw you back out again, and you know you're needed for the show this weekend," Cat laughed, secretly enjoying their ritual from her childhood.

"Okay, sweetheart, you need to go get the ladder so we can

get this sign up," Callum stopped King and let Cat slide off. "I'm also dying for that lemonade."

"Okay, daddy, I'll be right back," Cat told him.

"I love you, Kitty Cat," Callum called to her.

"I love you too, Daddy," Cat called over her shoulder as she ran from the room.

Cat ran through the stable. As she did, she could've sworn she heard raised voices coming from the arena. She turned to go back and find out what was happening when the stable manager, Luke, distracted her.

"Hi, Cat, are you okay?" Luke asked her. "You look a little breathless."

"Daddy needs the long ladder, and help with putting up the sign for the horse show," Cat told him. "Can you send one of the stable hands to help him, please?"

"I'll go. I just have to go to the storage block." Luke pulled a ring of keys off his belt. "Where are you off to now?"

"Daddy wants some of Bessie's lemonade." She looked up at him. "Would you like a glass?"

"I would love one." Luke walked with her to the kitchen door before veering off to go to the storage block.

Cat ran into the kitchen where Bessie was baking pies for the show.

"Hi, Kitty Cat," Bessie greeted her with a smile. "What can I get you?"

"Oh, no, Bessie. You carry on baking," Cat told her. "Daddy and Luke want some lemonade, and I'm quite capable of getting it."

"Okay honey," Bessie gave her a grateful smile. "I still have a load of goodies to bake." She plopped some dough onto the counter. "Can you believe that selfish cow tried to talk your daddy out of donating the proceeds of the horse show profits?"

"Don't worry, Daddy would never do that," Cat assured Bessie. She got the lemonade out of the refrigerator and put it on a tray with some glasses. "Can I please have some of your choc chip cookie dough?" She gave Bessie her sweetest smile.

"You know you make me cringe eating this stuff raw like this." Bessie shuddered. She cut off a piece of the dough and handed it to Cat. "You'd better eat this before you get back to your daddy. You know how he hates you eating this stuff."

"I'm eighteen now, Bessie," Cat reminded her. "He no longer has a say over what I eat."

"Oh, young lady, that's where you are so very wrong," Bessie warned her. "A parent always has a say in their kid's life no matter their age. Heck, I hated green beans, but whenever my momma was around, I made sure I ate everyone off my plate."

"Why didn't you just tell her you hated green beans," Cat asked.

"Because back then you ate whatever your parents put on your plate no matter your age," Bessie explained.

"That sounds like a bit of emotional child abuse and forcing a child to do something." Cat pointed out.

"Times were different back then, Kitty Cat," Bessie explained.

"Well, I'm glad I live in these modern times." Cat shook her head in disgust. "I couldn't imagine being forced to eat anything."

"Like I said, it was a different time." Bessie laughed. "One where kids actually listened to and respected their parents."

"Hey, I respect my parents." Cat picked up the tray. "Just not a certain step-parent."

"I think we can excuse you that one," Bessie told her.

"I'd better get this tray of drinks and snacks back to dad."

"Here, take some fresh baked cookies." Bessie put a whole lot of recently cooked cookies on a plate on the tray. "Now, don't you eat them all before you get there."

Cat laughed, picking a cookie up and taking a bite. "You know me so well." She kissed Bessie on the cheek and headed out the kitchen door.

Cat looked towards the store where Luke had taken four ladders out and he was looking them over. She rushed to the barn because she wanted to go up into the loft and see what the intruder had left there. Cat was going to gather up his things and drop them off at Chelsea's, so neither she nor her fling came back to Cupids Bow.

"Daddy, Bessie sent some of her freshly baked..." Cat had pushed the door open with her foot and nearly lost her balance when the door flew open.

Cat had barely managed to steady the tray when a figure blurred past her, pushing her flying. That time she did lose her balance and the tray when flying out of her hands. As the glasses crashed and splintered to the ground so did Cat's world. Crawling to her knees King's distressed call made her lift her head towards him and her heart stopped beating for a few seconds. At first, she could believe what she was seeing and stood staring dumbfounded at the sight before her.

"Daddy?" Cat called.

But her father's lifeless body dangled down King's side, who was trying very hard not to make any sudden moves as if he knew Callum was badly injured.

"DADDY!" Cat screamed, rushing forward, crunching over the broken glass.

Cat barely felt a piece slice into her exposed ankle. Nor did she feel the splinters of glass embedded in her palm. She reached her father and dropped down onto her knees where his head and shoulders were touching the ground.

"DADDY!" Cat shouted again. "Wake up." She felt for a pulse and breath from beneath his nose but there was nothing. "You must be doing it wrong, Cat." She said to air thin as she became more and more anxious when her father wasn't responding.

Her hands shook and unnoticed tears streamed down her cheeks as she tried to find a pulse once more, "Come on Daddy, I know you're still here. Please, you've got to still be here." Then she felt it. It was very faint, but it was there.

"Cat?" Winnie's voice had her head shooting up. "You!" Cat hissed. "You did this, didn't you?"

"Did what?" Winnie stood staring dumbfounded at Cat for a

few seconds before her eyes scanned the scene. "Callum?" She sounded like her voice was being ripped from her chest.

Winnie rushed forward to where Cat was now sitting cradling her father's head in her lap. There was no way she could lift Callum out of the awkward position he was in.

"Stay away!" Cat screamed at Winnie making her freeze as she glanced down at Cat.

"He's my husband, I have a right to be here!" Winnie screeched back. "Move!"

"Get Out!" Cat screamed back. "Get away from us."

"What in blazes is going..." Luke's eyes widened as she stepped around Winnie and saw Callum. "Callum!"

Luke pushed Winnie out of his way not caring that he nearly knocked her off her feet.

"Please, Luke, help him," Cat pleaded through her tears. "Help him."

Luke worked fast. As carefully as he could, he lifted Callum from King's side, who had been so patient and careful. Cat looked up and swallowed down nausea rising from her belly at the sight of all the blood staining the side of King's neck, the saddle, and down the horse's side. All Cat could think of was how calm the horse had been and how terrified when it had smelt Callum's blood. She sucked in a shaky breath.

Luke expertly felt Callum's body for breaks. "He's still alive, Cat." He tried to assure her. "Can you give me your jacket to put under your daddy's head?"

Cat nodded and took off her jacket. She folded it and gently put it beneath her father's head.

"Winnie, go call the emergency services," Luke barked out the order.

"But I want to be here with Callum." Winnie immediately started arguing. 'Send someone else."

Cat's eyes narrowed when she lifted her head and glared at Winnie. The woman was an excellent actress, but her cold eyes gave her true emotions away. Cat was convinced that the shrew felt nothing. She was probably already counting the pennies of her inheritance. Well, wasn't Winnie going to be in for a surprise. Cat knew that was the meanest thought she could have at a time like this. But Winnie was faking her emotions, which meant she was a suspect on Cat's list.

"What is going on?" One of the stable hands walked in and froze. "Mr. Sparrow!" He rushed forward.

"Clyde, go phone emergency services, now!" Luke barked and Clyde didn't argue he took off.

Cat's eyes scanned the scene to the door, where she was nearly knocked off her feet. In the dirt, she saw something shiny. Cat pushed herself to her feet but before she could get to the object Winnie had grabbed it and then pretended there was nothing there but glass.

"What was that?" Cat hissed.

"Glass, Cat," Winnie told her. "If you hadn't noticed there's a lot of it at the door entrance. I was merely trying to get it out of the way, so the emergency services didn't step on it."

"That wasn't glass," Cat said through gritted teeth. "Besides, the glass is all over there." She pointed to where the jugs and tumblers had crashed to the ground.

"Some of it must've shattered over here," Winnie's eyes narrowed. "You've had a huge shock. So, if you know what's good for you, you won't tell the police any of your imaginings."

Cat saw the warning flash in Winnie's mean eyes, and she knew that it was more of a threat than a warning. Winnie was hiding something. Then a thought crossed Cat's *mind. Was it Winnie who had knocked me flying when I came through the door?*

The emergency services and police arrived at the moment. The next few hours sped by in a blur of questions. Cat was the only one that was allowed to ride in the helicopter with Callum much to Winnie's disgust and ire. While a doctor patched up her wounds from the broken glass, the police had questioned Cat three times. Bessie had worked with Luke to call off the show for the weekend. Bessie and Luke were the only ones Cat would let near her. She'd demanded they keep Winnie away from her and told the police exactly what she'd seen Winnie do. But of course,

Winnie had spun some lies. Winnie had made the police believe Cat was trying to discredit her because she blamed Winnie for taking Callum's attention away from her.

The new week was terrible. Cat refused to leave Callum's side. He was lying lifeless on the bed in a coma with machines keeping him alive. Zac had arrived within a few hours of getting the news. He was the one that made Cat go home, shower, and eat. Then he'd bring her back to the hospital where Cat would spend her days reading to her father. She even discussed the journal with him in French, sure that he could hear her. By the end of the week when there was no improvement the doctors told them that they should think about letting Callum go. He was an organ donor, and there were a lot of lives he could save. Cat didn't want her father to save other people's lives. She wanted the doctors to save his life.

But Winnie the Angel of death decided to switch Callum's life support off. She told Cat rather coldly that if Callum couldn't breathe on his own, she was sure he didn't want to depend on machines to do so for him. Cat was furious and beside herself at how Zac and Winnie had tricked her out of Callum's room. Zac had told her he'd come to take her home to shower and have something to eat. So, Cat went with him trustfully. When they pulled up at the hospital was when Zac told her the truth that Winnie had the doctors turn off Callum's life support. Cat was so enraged and filled with pain that she lashed out and punched Zac in the nose. She'd sprained her hand and broken his nose.

But she didn't care. She jumped out of the car and ran through the hospital as fast as she could to get to her father's room. When she got there her father had already flat-lined and Winnie was signing the papers for the organ donations. Cat was already seeing red and not thinking straight. She'd flown into the room and attacked Winnie. Screaming at her that she was a murderer. It had taken three grown men to subdue Cat, and a hefty tranquilizer to knock her out. When she'd woken up, she was restrained to a hospital bed, and she had been bandaged up. Ashley, Holly, Bessie, and Rupert were all waiting by her bedside.

"Hi, honey," Bessie's gentle hands stroked the hair off Cat's forehead. "How are you feeling?"

"I want to go see my father," Cat said through clenched teeth. "Why am I restrained?"

"Kitty Cat you attacked your brother and Winnie," Rupert told her, stepping forward. "It took a lot of persuading for me to talk Winnie down from pressing charges."

"Did you remind her that she was a cold-blooded murderer?" Cat hissed. "I hate that woman. She'd better not be at my house when I get home."

"Ah," Rupert's eyes met Cat's and she knew that he too knew why she'd said that. "I see Callum managed to talk with you?"

"Yes," Cat said. "It also means that you're now my lawyer and you can no longer represent the Angel of death."

"Kitty Cat, you know I would only ever represent you or your family," Rupert assured her. "But sweetie you can't just ruthlessly kick Winnie out on the street because then you're no better than she is."

"I don't care!" Cat said through gritted teeth. Anger once again stained her cheeks red. "I want her gone, and I want Zac gone too."

"Cat!" Bessie said, shocked. "The decision to switch off your father's life support was out of Zac's hands, honey."

"He lied to me and manipulated me," Cat told her. "He's done nothing but take that witch's side since the day she sauntered into our lives. I want them both gone."

"Cat," Rupert told her patiently. "As I now represent you, you know I have to do what you wish me to do. But I implore you, sweetheart, to take a few hours to calm down and think about what your father would want you to do."

"That's a low blow," Cat told Rupert. "I'm thinking of firing you right now."

"Of course, you are," Rupert told her. "But you won't because I'm also your guardian until you're twenty-one." He pointed out.

"I'll emancipate myself from your guardianship then," Cat told him stubbornly. "After that, I'll fire you."

"Fair enough," Rupert said. "But in the meantime, as your lawyer might I suggest you take a few deep breaths and try not to attack anyone else for the next twenty-four hours?"

"Why twenty-four hours?" Cat asked him.

"It just seemed like an idea to give you a full day to work through all the emotions that must be churning inside," Rupert's voice was soft and full of compassion. "You know I'm always on your side, Kitty Cat." He squeezed her good hand gently.

"Fine," Cat said, lying back against the pillows. "But then you need to get me out of these confines, find my clothes, and get me in to see my father before they hack him apart to steal his organs."

"This is going to be a long night," Rupert sighed. "You three ladies, please keep an eye on her while I go see if I can carry out her wishes."

Chapter Eight

A SHOCK FOR ZAC - PART ONE

*P**resent Day*

"It's you!" Zack and Chelsea said together, then looked at each and smiled before looking at Cat.

"What's me?" Cat frowned.

"You're the owner of Cupids Bow," Zac said. "Chelsea and I have been trying to figure out who the mysterious owner was that Rupert couldn't tell us until they told us."

"It was a stipulation in daddy's will," Cat told them. "But why do you think that I own the ranch?"

"That night at the hospital when you attacked Winnie, you were lording it over all of us," Zac's eyes narrowed. "I didn't even think of it back then because I was reeling from having just lost dad."

"Zac actually just thought you were being a brat!" Chelsea admitted then looked at Zac innocently.

"Thanks a lot," Zac said, looking betrayed. "That was between you and me."

"Sorry, but I thought she needed to know the truth," Chelsea told him. "This is a day of truths, right?"

"That's okay, I thought Zac was an idiot back then," Cat admitted and gave Zac a smug smile. "I wanted to have you kicked off the ranch and never allowed back on it for doing what you did."

"Kitty Cat, I knew you'd never get out of the way for the doctor to do what he had to do," Zac's voice was low and gentle. "I hated betraying you the way I did. But in your heart, you know daddy would never have wanted to be kept alive by a machine."

"Yes, but neither of you had the right to take that choice away from me. Or to keep me from being at his side when he drew his last breath," Cat's eyes misted over. "I never even got to say goodbye to him."

"I'm so sorry, Kitty Cat." Zac's eyes were shadowed. "Your final fight with Winnie. You really could've kicked her out onto the street with nothing, couldn't you?"

"I was angry," Cat told Zac. "You, Chelsea, Winnie, and even Uncle Rupert had all ganged up on me. Trying to get me to go to that stupid university where you went."

"It's one of the top universities in the country," Zac told her. "We wanted you to be closer to home than Nashville on the other side of the country."

"Well, I wanted to go where I'd planned to go since I was ten," Cat said. "You and Winnie were trying to control me because you wanted to have numbers on your side if the owner of the ranch came to claim it."

"Only we didn't realize we were chasing the owner away!" Zac said softly. "And that's not why I wanted you to go to a university closer to home. I'd lost all my family except for you and you running off to Nashville made me feel like I was losing you too."

"You should've told me that back then, Zac." Cat sighed before asking. "Once again, why do you think I'm the owner of the ranch?"

"Oh, come on, Cat," Chelsea eyed her out. "You basically just admitted it to us in your story. Now you need to tell us. It's the truth's time remember?"

"I don't think this is the time or place to go down that truth alley," Cat warned them. "But to cut a long story about me leaving, short. After months of trying to live with Winnie constantly trying to sell things that weren't hers, like the ranch. She was planning on selling the ranch once she'd contested Dad's will. She wanted to flush the real owner out any way she could."

"She was really getting a bit much, even I have to agree," Zac said. "I actually think the settlement amount Dad left her was a pretty great sum to retire on and live a comfortable life."

"She would've breezed through that amount in a few months," Cat assured Zac. "It was only the threat from the bank manager that pulled her head out of the clouds. He was the one that made her realize there was no more money after that amount dried up."

"Oh, I'm sure she would've found a way to bleed some more money from us," Zac said and then frowned. "But she didn't." He looked at Chelsea. "She never asked us for any money after Cat left, did she?"

"No, only that we move her sister to Cupids Bow Ranch because she was supposed to be sick and frail." Chelsea rolled her eyes.

"I wonder why she stopped trying to sell the ranch or get more money from us?" Zac rubbed his chin thoughtfully.

"Probably because the bank manager got a legal letter that had been signed by daddy about a week before his so-called accident," Cat informed them. "Zac, daddy was about to serve Winnie with divorce papers. That's why he'd moved into the guest suit a week or so before the horse show and his accident."

"Excuse me?" Zac's brow drew into a deep frown. "How do you know this?

"Ashley found the letter that Rupert never had the chance to send. It was tucked away in daddy's client file," Cat explained. "She also found emails between Winnie and Rupert. Winnie was trying to get Rupert to let her know what was in Daddy's will."

"That shouldn't surprise you." Zac's eyes narrowed. "We all know how she hounded Rupert for that information practically from the moment of Dad's last breath."

"Zack," Cat said softly. "Winnie was bugging Uncle Rupert for the information a few days before Daddy's accident."

"Why are you only mentioning this now?" Zac hissed.

"No, Zac, I tried to tell you," Cat pointed out. "But you and Uncle Rupert, even the police as well, all just fobbed me off as a hysterical teenager who hated her stepmother."

"I'm so sorry, Kitty Cat," Zac's voice was hoarse with raw emotion. Chelsea could almost see the thoughts, guilt, and anger running through his mind. "I was so focused on trying to keep things from falling apart I couldn't see the struggle my little sister was going through."

"Only because I knew daddy had been murdered and no one, except Ashley and Bessie, took me seriously or helped me to try uncovering the truth," Cat told him.

"I thought you were obsessed with blaming someone for his accident," Zac's voice was filled with emotion. "What was I supposed to think, Kitty Cat? You closed down and shut us all out. You wouldn't even go into the stables. You stopped riding and if King was anywhere near you, you'd take off in a panic."

"I'm so sorry that I wasn't there for you, Cat." Chelsea swallowed down the burning lump in her throat as she diverted the conversation in a new direction. She could feel and see that they were both getting too emotional. Chelsea also didn't want to remember the day of Callum's accident.

"No, Chels, I know you tried on many occasions to reach out." Cat gave her a sad smile. "I know it was you that left those little gifts for me to find. You knew how much those little treasures made me smile."

"I wanted to see you smile again," Chelsea told her honestly. "I wanted to try and help you through the pain. I remember how it cut you up when your mom died." Her eyes misted over. "I could only imagine the pain you were feeling over the horror you went through."

"Thank you, Chels," Cat said, her voice also hoarse with emotion. "You have no idea how many times I wanted to write you a little thank you card or letter."

"Cat, Dad's death was ruled an accident." Zac derailed Chelsea's plans to steer the conversation away from whether or not their father had been murdered. "Why were you so adamant it wasn't?"

"It wasn't an accident," Cat told them. "I saw Harris rush through the doors of the arena before I found daddy." She looked directly at Chelsea. "He has always been my first prime suspect."

"Cat, why would Harris kill your father?" Chelsea asked, feeling just as confused now as she had been when Cat had accused her of aiding and abetting a murderer.

"First of all, do you remember when he was bad-mouthing my mother at school that day?" Cat asked Chelsea.

"Yes." Chelsea nodded.

"We wondered who he got so upset about that we were indirectly calling a bitter liar?" Cat looked at Chelsea who nodded. "It was his mother."

"His mother?" Chelsea was shocked. "How did she know your mother?"

"They all went to school together," Cat told Chelsea. "But you already know this. Don't you, Chelsea?"

"How would I know who his mother is?" Chelsea denied Cat's accusation. "He never mentioned the woman to me."

"You know I always wondered why when you and Zac hit me with your engagement the day I left, you always took Winnie's side." Chelsea didn't like the look in Cat's eyes.

"I'm still not following you," Chelsea said.

"Then there was also the way you defended Harris when you set him up as a squatter in Cupids Bow Ranch's stables." Cat gave a brittle laugh. "You even told me Zac knew he was staying there and that it was his idea."

"When did I tell you to put Harris Conway up in the stables?" Zac asked Chelsea.

"I didn't," Chelsea said defensively. "The only person I put up in your barn was..." Realization suddenly dawned, and Chelsea and she turned to Cat. "That's why you laid into me the day of your father's accident. You thought that guy staying in your stables was Harris?"

"Chelsea, I had just caught you at the creek with Harris," Chelsea pointed out. "Who else could it have been."

"It wasn't Harris," Chelsea told her. "And I was at the creek on my own waiting for the guy who was staying in your stables when Harris showed up out of the blue."

"Why would he do that?" Cat asked her suspiciously.

"He said he came to meet with his Aunt," Chelsea shrugged. "I told him he'd better get off your land before a Sparrow or one of their ranch workers saw him."

"That's not what I witnessed," Cat told Chelsea. "You were in his arms."

"Ah..." Zac nodded. "I can see why that would've looked like it did." He started to laugh. "Oh, my beautiful, protective, and fast-to-jump-to-conclusions little sister."

"What's so funny?" Cat scoffed. "Chelsea was cheating on you with Harris."

"Okay maybe the date," Zac looked at Chelsea and she knew she had some explaining to do. "But Chelsea slipped on the rocks and Harris grabbed her to stop her from a dangerous fall."

"Is that what she told you?" Cat asked him.

"No, it's what David Miller told me," Zack said.

"David Miller?" It was Cat's turn to frown.

"Cat, it wasn't Harris who was shacking up in our stables, it was David," Zac told her. "I asked Chelsea to help him sneak in and out of the ranch."

"That was David who was in the office while dad and I were talking in the arena?" Cat's eyes were wide with shock.

"Yes," Zac confirmed.

"Was it also David who dashed out of the arena when I found dad?" Cat asked.

"No," Chelsea frowned. "David was at Mountain Rise when that happened." She told Cat. "When you went off to the ranch house I slipped back into the stables and got David's things."

"Do you know if he can speak French?" Cat looked at Zac.

"As far as I know he's fluent in quite a few languages including French," Zac told her.

Chelsea watched Cat's eyes widen and her face pale. *What were Cat and Callum speaking about in French that they didn't want anyone else to hear?* Now Chelsea was curious about what Cat and Callum were speaking about that day.

"Did you see anyone else in the arena while you were in the offices?" Cat asked Chelsea.

Chelsea felt shockwaves zing through her fingertips. Memories of the day Callum had his accident flashed through her mind. Her heart started to beat in her chest as she knew the secret she'd been carrying with her for all these years was about to come out. A strange sense of dread mixed with relief flooded her.

"I saw someone in a dark gray or charcoal color hoodie," Chelsea admitted feeling good to tell someone that burden she'd been carrying around all these years. "I only got a glimpse of his face, but I hadn't seen him before until the day Hayden got beaten up at the Creek."

"Who was it?" Cat asked her.

"The man looked a lot like Ron Hicks' oldest son," Chelsea told them. "When I met the boy who'd beaten up my son, he looked so familiar. It wasn't until a lot later when I walked into the Cupids Bow arena a few days later that it dawned on. The boy looked a lot like the man I saw with your father in the arena that day."

"You think it was Ron Hicks in the arena with my father?" Cat's brows creased.

"Yes," Chelsea nodded. "He burst into the arena giving me such a fright. Then when your father and he started arguing I knew it was time to get out of there."

"Chelsea, did you see what happened?" Cat asked her.

"No," Chelsea shook her head. "Like I said I ducked down when I heard the man crash through the arena doors. I did peek again before I left to make sure they were still in the arena so I could make my escape."

"Did you notice if he was wearing a belt buckle?" Cat looked at Chelsea.

"I honestly couldn't tell you. But I did notice he was holding something silver in his hands because he was twirling it around," Chelsea said. "I couldn't get a good look at it. I wasn't actually trying to. All I wanted to do was escape before I got caught."

"Did you see anyone else in or near the arena?" Zac asked her.

"No, but when I was walking out of the stables Winnie appeared behind me out of nowhere," Chelsea told them. "She was looking at me in a rather suspicious way and asked me what I was doing there. So, I lied and told her that I was getting some clothes Ashley left in Turin's stall."

"You're only telling us this now?" Cat said in disbelief.

"None of it seemed relevant at the time," Chelsea told her. "I didn't hear of your father's accident until the next day. And if it had been ruled out, what I'd seen didn't seem relevant nor was I thinking of it when I heard the news about your father."

"But you told the police you didn't see or hear anything," Cat pointed out. "In fact, I think you told them that you went straight home after our run-in."

"I was trying to protect David," Chelsea explained.

"Why was David even staying in our stable?" Cat asked, looking confused. "Weren't his parents rich?"

"David got into a bit of trouble," Zac told Cat. "He was framed for beating up this girl he'd taken on a date."

"He did what?" Cat's eyes widened as she gave her brother a sideways look.

"He didn't beat the girl up," Chelsea defended David.

"That's what all abusers say," Cat said.

"No, Cat he couldn't have been the one who did it," Chelsea told her. "Because David was with Zac and me on the night the girl was beaten."

"Only the cops wouldn't believe our story because we're David's friends," Zac continued the story. "He needed a place to lay low until his brother could help him find the evidence, they needed to clear David's name."

"He nearly lost everything because of that accusation," Chelsea told Cat.

"Oh," was all Cat said. But something flickered in Cat's eyes.

"It couldn't have been David in the arena with your dad either because he was at my house with my parents," Chelsea informed Cat. "It wasn't Harris either because someone had him arrested for trespassing." She raised her eyebrows at Cat.

"It wasn't me," Cat told them honestly. "Although that's the best thing I've heard in a while."

"I have to say I agree," Zac said. "Kitty Cat, why do you think dad didn't have an accident?"

"The way he'd fallen and the gash on the back of his head," Cat explained. "When Luke looked at it, it looked weird like it had patterns in the mark. Nowhere on the wall or the floor were there patterns like that or any blood marks to say he'd hit his head somewhere. How would he have hit his head like that on the back of his horse?"

"Now that I think of it, it did look like someone had bashed him over the head," Zac said thoughtfully.

"Also, the blood patterns on King," Cat told them. "The hair on King's body that was coated in blood looked like Dad had been dragged up onto the horse. If he'd fallen in the position, he had..."

"The hair would be smoothed downward and smeared with blood," Chelsea deduced. "You also said there was blood all over King's neck and his hindquarters."

"Yes, like daddy had been pushed into the saddle. His body had fallen face-first onto King's neck."

"King would've become antsy smelling the blood," Chelsea continued. "The horse probably did a bit of a jump or prance. Your dad was unconscious so he fell backward, and his head would hit the hindquarters."

"That's how the blood was transferred onto King. Then his body twisted around before sliding down in the position I found him in," Cat sucked in a shaky breath. "His one leg was caught in the saddle and his other leg in the stirrup."

"So, how do the police think he'd had an accident like that?" Chelsea asked, perplexed.

"They said he must have bashed his head when he hit the ground," Cat said, disgusted.

"Now that you tell me this it does sound as if they didn't do much investigating." Zac rubbed his chin thoughtfully.

"I think the police were paid off," Cat told them.

"Kitty Cat, that's quite an accusation to make," Zac said. "You have to have proof of these things."

"A few days after daddy's accident I got a call from his bank manager." Cat bit her bottom lip. "He asked me if I could come into the bank. He was also very specific that I came there alone."

"That's a rather strange request!" Chelsea said.

"It was because daddy had become suspicious of Winnie's motives for marrying him," Cat explained. "He had the bank manager cut down Winnie's allowance two days before his accident. She'd drawn a huge sum of money out of her account and had asked the bank manager if he could advance her a bit of her next month's money."

"That's weird," Zac said with a frown. "She got a lot of money each month. I was amazed when Bessie told me that dad was always having to top it up for her because she spent it so quickly."

Cat shook her head. "Apparently, Winnie told both daddy and the bank manager she was helping her sick sister."

"I'm sorry but her sister was not sick," Chelsea said. "When she moved in here Zac, and I were expecting her to be so frail. She was anything but. In fact, she was a bigger shrew than Winnie was."

"And so bitter." Zac looked at Chelsea and smiled, making her heart skip a few beats once again. "You were so good with her though."

"Nursing training!" Chelsea raised her eyebrows and shook her head. "We learn how to deal with difficult patients."

"Oh, yes I had the pleasure of meeting her," Cat shocked them by saying.

"When did you meet Winnie's sister?" Zac looked at Cat, surprised.

"Not in person, but she called me," Cat told them. "The day before I left the ranch."

"Why didn't you say anything?" Zac looked at her.

"Because you were too busy consoling the enemy," Cat said. "And I really thought Chelsea knew exactly who Harris's mother was. You know I thought about coming to tell you what I had found out about Winnie after she and her sister left the ranch for good."

"Why didn't you?" Zac asked her.

"We can get back to that reason," Cat told him.

"Cat, when did you meet Winnie's sister?" Chelsea asked her.

"The day before I left Cupids Bow for good, I had the displeasure of meeting her sister." Cat looked at Chelsea and then Zac.

Zac looked at Cat curiously. "Why didn't you tell me?"

"Like I said it wasn't in person she phoned me." Cat looked at her purse propped up against the armchair she was sitting in.

"Why would she do that?" Chelsea asked, curiously. "I was so sorry that I helped Zac decide to let that woman move in here for as long as she did."

"She really wasn't a nice person," Zac told Cat. "We were expecting this frail ill woman. She was anything but frail or ill."

"I was about to come clean to you about everything," Cat told Zac. "I wanted to make you understand why I wanted to go to Nashville and not the university you were trying to force me to."

Cat looked from Chelsea to Zac and Chelsea could see there was a struggle going on inside Cat. There was something she was keeping from them and right now Cat was warring with herself about whether to let them know or not.

"Cat, why do I get the feeling you've been keeping a vital part of the puzzle to yourself?" Zac took Chelsea's same thoughts and voiced them.

"The day before I left, I made the mistake of telling Bessie that I was thinking of taking another six months sabbatical before going to Nashville and Aunt Simone," Cat told them.

"You told Bessie everything, so I don't see that as a mistake," Zac smiled at Cat reassuringly. "Trust me, Bessie would never betray your confidence."

"No, you were like a daughter to her," Chelsea confirmed Zac's statement. "She was fiercely protective and loyal to you."

"I know." Cat nodded. "My mistake was having the conversation with Bessie in the kitchen where Winnie could lurk around the corners." She shook her head. "Apparently, she overhead us and went running to her sister. I think she knew I'd throw the spanner in their plan for her sister to move here so they could work a way to get the ranch."

"She heard what you and Bessie were talking about," Chelsea guessed. "That woman was always lurking around corners. Her sister was even worse!"

"I have to agree with you, Chelsea." Cat smiled at Chelsea. "It was after my conversation with Bessie that I decided to lay down the law with Winnie. After all, I knew she wasn't supposed to be at Cupids Bow anymore. So did she."

"I remember that day," Zac told Cat. "Very well in fact. I nicknamed the day the showdown at Cupids Bow!"

"I arrived in the middle of that showdown." Chelsea blew out a breath. "I wanted to turn and run right back out of the front door."

"But I stopped her." Zac raised his hand. "Chelsea and I were supposed to announce our engagement that day. You kinda overshadowed our happy news."

"You should've warned me about the engagement then and not blindsided me after I'd had my eruption with the step monster." Cat raised her eyebrows pointedly.

"Cat you weren't talking to me or Chelsea!" Zac's voice was filled with exasperation.

"You could've told Bessie," Cat said with a shrug. "You know she would've told me."

"Can we get back to the conversation?" Chelsea gently steered the two of them off another volatile path. She and Cat were just starting to mend bridges. She didn't want to have to take sides between her ex-best friend or ex-husband.

"Sorry," Cat apologized to Chelsea. "As you know I went and confronted Winnie. I told her that she had a week to pack her bags and get the heck off my land."

"I can remember that because you were very loud about it," Zac told Cat.

"She then sneered at me and told me that she was Callum's widow and had every right to be there," Cat went over that conversation. "That's when I assured her, I had proof that they weren't going to be married for much longer if daddy were still alive."

"That's when she said, well he isn't." Chelsea could remember that conversation as clear as day. "If only she'd stopped there."

"Instead, she told Cat that no little girl was going to stand in her way of getting what she wanted or kicking her off a ranch that was soon going to be hers to do what she wanted with." Zac sighed and shook his head. "She didn't stop there either."

"Nope, instead she threw it in Cat's face that she was going to sell the land to a developer who was going to tear it down piece by piece." Chelsea shuddered remembering what happened next.

"That's when I punched her," Cat admitted.

"You could've just slapped her, Kitty Cat," Zac said. "But no, you had to punch her. Hard. Right in the stomach."

"Well, the last time I punched someone in the face I had to have stitches and I bruised my hand badly," Cat said. "So, I figured that the stomach would be softer and wouldn't hurt me."

"But you made matters so much worse for us because she had something over us," Zac explained. "One of the main reasons we moved her dreadful sister into Cupids Bow was to keep Winnie from laying charges against you."

"She could've tried," Cat told them. "By then, I had gathered quite a bit of evidence against her, her sister, and Harris."

"Harris didn't kill your father!" Chelsea said once again.

"I didn't know that then," Cat pointed out. "Just before all of you ran into the living room screaming at me, I gave Winnie two days to pack her things and get out. I warned her that if she didn't or if she tried to come after my family I would go straight to the police."

"We didn't hear that!" Zac admitted.

"Yes, but then she got up and put on one of her great performances for all of you," Cat remembered. "Once again you all turned your back on me and took the witch's side." She squeezed her eyes shut. "Even Bessie turned on me that day. I was so angry I stormed off and called the bank manager and froze all of your accounts. Then I called Rupert and told him to start drawing up formal eviction notices for all of you."

"Thanks!" Zac breathed. "Nice to know my own sister was about to evict me from my home."

"Well, you were all trying to push me out of my home," Cat told them. "Well, at least that's what it seemed like to me. I was all alone trying to fight this battle for my father and Cupids Bow but none of you seemed to care. You were all just rallying around the witch."

"There are no words to express my remorse over what we did to you." Zac's eyes were shadowed. "Kitty Cat, why didn't you go ahead and serve those notices on us?"

"Two reasons," Cat stated. "First, when I cooled off, I realized how irrational I'd been. It was only Winnie I wanted gone. Second, Winnie's delightful sister called me and threatened me."

"What on earth could she have threatened you with?" Chelsea asked before Zac could.

"Don't worry I threatened her back, I told her I knew exactly who she and Winnie were." Cat's eyes sparked with anger. "But then she threw me a curveball that swallowed the wind from my sails leaving me stranded. She knew something about our family that I never thought Daddy told anyone, least of all Winnie."

"Are you talking about the reason why dad didn't leave Cupids Bow to me or gave me the land guardianship?" Zac's eyes narrowed.

"I..." Cat swallowed nervously. "Zac..." She bit her lower lip and her eyes flashed with worry. "I'm sorry but now really is not the time."

"No, I want to know," Zac insisted. "First you get the family heirloom journal and the story of the guardianship of the land. A story I as the firstborn should've got. Now I found out that you're the heir of Cupids Bow."

Chelsea watched Cat swallow and pinch the bridge of her nose. She knew that pose in Cat well. It meant there was something she was keeping from them. Something Cat didn't want to tell them because she hated hurting the people she loved. If Cat had kept this secret since she was eighteen it meant that it was crippling information.

"Zac, maybe we should let Cat finish her story of why she left?" Chelsea said, giving his hand a quick squeeze.

The moment Chelsea touched Zac's hand she'd know it was a mistake. That old electric shock every time they touched when they were younger shot up her arm.

"No, Chels," Zac said to her. "I appreciate the consideration, but I need to know what is going on. I'm supposed to be the rightful heir of the land but, for some reason, my father cut me off."

"No, Zac," Cat said softly, shaking her head. "Daddy didn't purposely cut you off."

"Then why are you the heir and not me..." He stopped and his eyes widened in realization. "You really are the heir, aren't you?" He looked at Cat wide-eyed. "That's why Indy has the Sparrow last name and not Lockran."

"Zac!" Cat didn't want to have this conversation. "Dad wanted with all his heart for you to be his rightful heir and for us to share everything. But he couldn't do it because of his promise. He also knew that I would always give you the full run of the ranch as if it was yours."

"So, you are the mysterious heir then!" Zac looked at Cat with hurt shining in his eyes. "Why couldn't dad leave the ranch to me, Cat?"

Chelsea's heart went out to him. She wanted to put her arms around him and hold him. But she knew he'd probably not be receptive to that. Especially not today when he'd found out about Harris and why he didn't inherit his beloved Cupids Bow Ranch.

"Because he didn't know if you were his son or not," Cat said so softly that both Chelsea and Zac thought they'd heard things at first.

"What?" Both Chelsea and Zac choked.

Chapter Nine

A SHOCK FOR ZAC - PART TWO

"Did you know about this?" Zac asked Chelsea, looking at her accusingly.

"No, Cat and I haven't spoken in years. The last time she even addressed me directly was in the barn the day of your father's accident," Chelsea told him. "Then again, a few weeks ago the day my mother passed away."

"What do you mean he didn't know if I was his son or not?" Zac asked Cat.

Chelsea breathed a sigh of relief that he believed that she hadn't known this.

Cat picked up her purse and pulled out an envelope. "The night I left Bessie gave me a letter from dad. I opened it on the plane to Nashville." She patted the envelope in her hands once she'd put her purse back down. "The night dad took me to dinner he told me that there was a very good reason why Zac wasn't being given the guardianship of Cupids Bow."

"So, you knew he had doubts about me being his son from back then?" Zac looked even more hurt and betrayed.

"No," Cat told him honestly. "I didn't. And Daddy didn't elaborate on the reason why that night either." She leaned forward looking down at the letter. "I didn't know until I read

this. At first, it didn't make much sense to me. I had to read it a
few times and then asked Maria what she made of it."

"Maria Parker knows about this?" Zac hissed in disbelief.
"Wow! So that means Brett knows too."

"No!" Cat said with conviction. "Maria would never say a
word to anyone."

"That makes me feel so much better!" Zac's voice dripped
with hurt and sarcasm.

"Here." Cat gave Zac the letter.

Zac took it and looked at the envelope. It was addressed to
Cat. He passed it to Chelsea asking, "Would you mind?"

Chelsea smiled and her heart skipped a beat. When Zac
couldn't face what was in a letter, he'd asked Chelsea to read it to
him. He said that hearing it from her lips softened the blow or
made good news more exciting for him.

"Of course," Chelsea said, giving his leg a compassionate pat.
She looked in the thick A4 envelope. "There are two letters in
here." She pulled out the opened one and straightened the paper.

Dear Kitty Cat,

*I've asked Bessie to give this letter to you when the time is right and if
you're reading it, it means my suspicions were right after all. I'm glad we
got to have the talk about the land on your eighteenth birthday. You have
no idea how long I've agonized over what I was going to say. My father
made the official handing over of the guardianship so fascinating and he
made me feel like the most important person in the world. I wanted to
make you feel the same way. To know that Cupids Bow was neither a
burden nor a curse but an honor to be a part of.*

*The land, as you must now know, is steeped in mystery, history, and if you
honor it, riches. My father told me it was both a blessing and sometimes a
curse but if you pushed through the hardships, you'd come out the other
side rich beyond your wildest dreams. As you know, being rich doesn't
always mean physical riches, it means riches of the soul. To enjoy great
wealth, you need to be a humble being with a rich soul. I tried to teach*

these lessons to both you and your brother but as my father told me the journey of self is not one that can be taught it has to be experienced. This is now yours and your brother's journey to experience, learn from, and I hope with all I am, that you return from all the richer.

I have always taught you and your brother not to keep secrets that could harm a person to yourself. After reading this letter you're both going to see that as rather hypocritical of me. But there is a difference between protecting someone or simply hiding things from someone. The secret I kept was not mine to tell or mine to dig into. That was something that had to be between your mother and Zac. She was going to talk to Zac when he turned sixteen but as you know she never made it to Zac's sixteenth birthday. I made her a promise to let fate decide when or where Zac's secret was to be revealed. That is when she gave me the second envelope you will find with this letter. A truth that was between me and Zac. A truth I got to choose what to do with.

I chose my own truth. I didn't care if Zac was of my blood or not. He is and always will be my son, my family, my boy, and one of my biggest pride and joys. I didn't need a piece of paper to tell me that. So now I make it your truth, sweet, Kitty Cat. As the guardian of the sacred land, you're now the keeper of your mother's and my secret. You may think this an easy choice to make but trust me it is not. There are always two paths to every dilemma in life. It's up to you which one you choose to take. But this is not one of those choices like do I go for the green shoes or the blue shoes. This is a choice about a person's life. Do you derail it, or do you keep letting it run on the tracks it has been running perfectly fine on all these years?

I had my reason for my decision, but they can't be your reason, Kitten. I have every faith in you to make the right one and not a snap one. The easiest path to take may seem like the best choice because it is less fuss, and less troublesome. But that's only less fuss and trouble for you because your path is cleared. It's the other person's path you have to think about as well though. Because your decision doesn't only affect your journey; it affects your brother's too. Travel safely, my little princess, and I know

When Chelsea looked up at Zac his eyes were misted with tears as were hers.

"What is the other letter?" Zac's voice was hoarse with emotion.

"I don't think that's for me to tell you." Chelsea handed the envelope to Cat before Zac could take it from her. "Like the letter said, it is Cat's decision to give it to you."

Cat took the envelope and looked inside it at the unopened letter. "One of the main reasons I left that night is because Winnie's sister called me that day and told me I had a choice to make: get out of her sister's way or have Zac find out the truth."

"Winnie's sister got to you like that?" Zac looked at Cat startled. "Why didn't you come forward with this sooner?"

"I was hurting," Cat told him. "And you didn't seem to care. All you cared about was making sure Winnie was comfortable and kept happy. You refused to open your eyes and see the torture she inflicted on me each day I was at the ranch under the same roof as her."

"Oh, Kitty Cat, I'm so sorry." Zac wiped his eyes. "I felt so guilty about not being there for you or dad. I was obsessed with helping Winnie because that's one I could control." He shook his head. "I also thought that maybe dad had left everything to her and there was no way I was going to lose Cupids Bow to her."

"Not to mention, Zac was trying to keep Winnie from laying more charges against you," Chelsea defended Zac.

"I could've handled Winnie," Cat assured them. "What I couldn't handle, even though I was mad at you, was that you found out that I was the heir to Cupids Bow." She looked at Zac with misty eyes. "I didn't know back then about dad not knowing if you were his son or not. I thought the woman meant she knew I was the sole Cupids Bow heir."

"But that wasn't the threat, right?" Zac looked at the unopened envelope Cat pulled out of the bigger one.

"No." Cat handed Zac the unopened envelope. "I found out a few months after I arrived in Nashville that Winnie's sister was a lab tech."

Chelsea looked at the envelope in Zac's hand and instantly knew what was inside there. It was DNA results.

"This envelope is dated nineteen-eight-four," Chelsea's head shot up and she looked at Cat. "That was the year your mother passed away."

"Yes, and if you look at the name on the envelope, you'll see it was addressed to my mother," Cat pointed out. "It was mom who ordered the DNA test, not dad."

"She wanted dad to have the choice of knowing or not," Zac's voice was low. "And he never opened it."

"No," Cat confirmed and shook her head. He looked at Chelsea. "What should we do?"

Chelsea swallowed. She knew it was not the best time for her heart to be going wild and the long-dormant butterflies to suddenly come awake flapping in excitement. But Zac hadn't looked at her like that or included her in a family decision since she'd walked out on their marriage fourteen years ago. She had to stop her hands from trembling when she reached out and took the envelope from him.

"I think I should open it," Chelsea made the decision for

both Zac and Cat. "Then the burden of the secret becomes mine to bear. After that I say we burn the document. Then the two of you can decide what you want me to do with this secret."

"We can't put that on you, Chels." Cat looked at her with shadowed eyes.

"Cat's right." Zac's warm hand closed over Chelsea's, accelerating her heart even more. "You've got so much on your plate right now."

"Trust me." Chelsea gave his hand a gentle squeeze. "I could use the distraction. Besides you and Cat are my family."

"What do you think, Cat?" Zac looked at her sister.

"I think if Chelsea wants to see the results we should let her," Cat told him. "We need to put all this uncertainty to bed once and for all."

"What if I am his son?" Zac asked Cat. "What happens to the land then?"

"I asked Rupert and he told me that Daddy didn't disclose that secret to him," Cat said. "Rupert said that the person with Dad's last wishes will come forward once they knew Zac knew the truth."

"Why wouldn't your father want Rupert to know his last wishes?" Chelsea frowned. "They were the best of friends."

"Uncle Rupert said that Dad had grown paranoid in the last few weeks of his life," Cat told them. "I remember when Winnie was away visiting her sister. That first night dad moved all the trunks and valuables from the attic to somewhere."

"Yes, we've never been able to find that stuff," Zac said.

"Apparently, that's not all Daddy hid either," Cat explained. "He hid some treasures for a friend of his too."

"How strange," Zac frowned. "Do you think Dad and this friend knew about all this trouble before it started? Or that someone was trying to kill him?"

"Oh, so now you think his death wasn't an accident?" Cat looked at her brother in disbelief.

"I'm saying you have a point about his accident," Zac told her.

"Okay, the both of you!" Chelsea interrupted their conversation. "Let's get back to this letter."

Cat and Zac both looked at Chelsea and nodded.

"I'm opening it." Before anyone could say another word, Chelsea ripped open the envelope.

Chelsea stood up and walked into the kitchen before she pulled the document out. She was a qualified nurse practitioner and had learned a long time ago how to read blood work results. Chelsea took a deep breath and opened the document. She stood staring at the results. Little tingles of nerves zapped through her fingers and made her heart thud once again.

Schooling herself not to react, she calmly folded the letter and shoved it into her jeans pocket to get rid of later. Chelsea took another deep breath, squared her shoulders, and walked calmly back into the living room. Zac and Cat were staring at her expectantly.

"Well?" Zac asked. "Am I a Sparrow or not?"

Chelsea looked at Cat, "You both need to agree to want to know the results."

Zac looked questioningly at his sister, "Cat?"

Cat's eyes widened as she looked at Zac, "Are you sure you want to know, big brother? Because if you do then I say Chelsea must tell us. But like Daddy warned, this could completely derail your life, Zac."

"Kitty, Cat, my life is already derailed from today's conversation anyway." Zac gave her a small smile. "My life was derailed when I lost both of my parents and then learned I didn't inherit anything but a bank account." He gave a small self-mocking laugh and looked at Cat. "That was such a blow learning the land we love. Our home wasn't ours."

"I'm sorry I couldn't tell you anything, Zac," Cat's eyes once again misted over. "I had to make a promise to dad."

"I understand, Kitty Cat," Zac assured her. "But now, this is my truth and I need to know."

"Okay," Cat nodded. "But whatever it is. You are my brother."

"I know," Zac smiled and looked at Chelsea. "We want to know."

"Okay, then," Chelsea said, pulling the results from her pocket. "Zac, I can say that you are indeed a Sparrow."

"Are you sure?" Zac's eyes were wide and misty.

"One hundred percent sure." Chelsea handed him the results.

"Oh, thank goodness!" Cat's features reflected her relief.

Cat jumped out of her chair and rushed over to her brother, hugging him without caring that tears were spilling over her lids.

"That was intense." Zac's voice was hoarse, and he swiped at his eyes as he hugged Cat.

"I know," Cat said, stepping back and smiling at Chelsea. "I thought you were going to do one of those game show pause things."

"Oh, no!" Chelsea joked. "I know how angry you get, and I really didn't want to be the third person you punched in your lifetime."

Cat and Zac laughed at Chelsea's joke, which broke the last bit of tension in the room.

"So, do you think a magic elf will pop out of the walls with Daddy's last wishes?" Cat asked, grinning, as she plopped back into the armchair she'd been sitting in.

"I don't know," Zac said. "Do we call Ashley maybe now that she handles all our legal work?"

"She's not too happy with me," Cat admitted. "I haven't been the nicest person to her as of late."

"I feel that's my fault," Chelsea said apologetically.

"No," Cat denied. "It's mine. I got so busy with my career and life in Nashville that I neglected my Montana life."

"That's true," Zac rubbed it in. "If we didn't contact you, I doubt whether we'd ever hear from you."

"Might I suggest we don't burn that document?" Cat pointed to the DNA results that Zac was still holding. "We need them for that magic elf when it shows up."

"True," Zac agreed and handed the document back to Cat.

"As you've been looking after it for so long. I think you should keep it until the elf appears."

"Good thinking," Cat said, taking the letter from Zac and putting them all back in her purse.

"Now that that intense moment is over," Chelsea said. "I think we need some more refreshments."

"Yes, because now it's time for your story." Cat gave her a sweet smile.

"Yes, but mine isn't that long," Chelsea teased Cat.

"Then maybe on another day, we might get the scoop on what really happened between you and your second ex-husband," Zac told Cat.

"That's not a story I'm ready to tell anyone quite yet," Cat told them honestly. "It is still rather raw for me. Not the break up but he did to my career."

"I bet your first husband is going to have a field day with that when he arrives here," Zac said.

"Paul Lockran is coming back to Cupids Bow?" Chelsea looked at Cat in shock. "Why?"

"He says he needs a place to lay low for a while because of his soon-to-be ex-wife." Cat shrugged. "I don't really know. I'm just glad that West will be staying at Big Valley when Paul arrives."

"Oh no," Chelsea said. "So, the brothers are going to her at the same time?"

Cat nodded. "And they still haven't made up. West hasn't spoken to Paul in all these years."

"Yikes!" Chelsea winced. "When do they arrive?"

"West should be here today or tomorrow. I'm not sure when Paul is arriving." Cat stood up and started gathering the coffee pot, tray, and mugs. "I'll go make the coffee."

Cat disappeared into the kitchen leaving Zac and Chelsea alone in the living room. Chelsea didn't know why but she suddenly felt a little shy and nervous. Which was ridiculous because she and Zac had been married for seventeen years. For the last fourteen they'd been divorced, they'd shared the kids and been in contact many times. She shook that feeling off.

"Sorry we hijacked you today," Zac said, smiling at her.

"It's not a problem, I think we all needed this," Chelsea admitted. "Cat came to see me on the most unfortunate day. Since then, she's been at my house every day helping me."

"I wonder what she wants?" Zac looked thoughtful.

"What could Cat possibly want from me?" Chelsea asked him. "She's a star for goodness sake."

"I don't know," Zac said. "But she and David are spending an awful lot of time together lately. I know they are plotting something."

"Or maybe you're just being paranoid!" Chelsea shook her head. "She hasn't had a chance to talk to me yet."

"You wanted to see me?" Zac looked at her questioningly.

"It can wait," Chelsea told him.

"No, Cat's going to be a while," Zac told her. "She took her phone with her. I think she needed to make some calls."

"I don't quite know how to say what I need to say to you," Chelsea admitted. "In my head, I rehearsed it over and over again. But then Cat answered the door and completely threw me."

"Well, just say the first thing that pops into your head," Zac advised. "It seems to work for our kids and Cat." He smiled and it nearly bowled her over. It lit up his handsome features.

What is wrong with me? Chelsea admonished herself. *Get a grip, you're not some hormonal teenager!*

"I need your help," Chelsea blurted it out. She stopped and frowned. "Wow, that really does work!"

"I told you!" Zac gave her a teasing smile. "You know I'm always here for you, Chels." His voice dipped a little lower

"I know," Chelsea acknowledged. "I know I have absolutely no right to ask. But I'm in deep trouble and I can't afford to lose the last of my legacy. I would really like to pass Mountain Rise onto our kids one day."

"That sounds so strange to say," Zac told her. "Our ancestors couldn't be too happy with us having Sparrow and Hitchin blood mixed now."

"You had to throw your Sparrow name in there somewhere, didn't you?" Chelsea laughed.

"For the first time in a long time I really appreciate my family name," Zac admitted. "I guess I never knew my paternal parentage was ever in question, so it was just a given."

"But when you thought it was being ripped away from you, you realize just how much your family name and blood mean to you," Chelsea finished for him.

"Exactly," Zac said. "Wow what would've happened if I weren't a Sparrow?"

"Nothing," Chelsea assured him. "As your father said, you were always his son. He never needed a DNA test to prove it."

"Yes, but I didn't get Cupids Bow or the guardianship of the land legacy," Zac pointed out.

"Zac, you know your father took all that land guardianship very seriously," Chelsea reminded him. "Like Cat said, it broke his heart not to be able to hand Cupids Bow over to both you and her."

"My sister really could've kicked us all off Cupids Bow!" Zac ran his hand through his hair. "She wasn't joking about that."

"But she didn't," Chelsea told him. "She left instead."

"Only because Winnie's sister threatened her and..." Zac trailed off. He frowned. "Pass me Cat's bag."

"I'm not going to let you go through a woman's purse." Chelsea pulled away and gave him a disapproving stare. "That's sacred space."

"No, I want to see the DNA report." Zac started to push himself awkwardly into a standing position.

"Stay!" Chelsea pointed at him like she did to Major, their Great Dane. "I'll get it."

"Is Major still giving you discipline issues?" Zac asked her.

"He's been impossible since he came back from his holiday with you," Chelsea told him, reaching over to pull the envelope from Cat's bag. "You're the one who wanted this and gave me permission to dig in your sister's purse if she asks."

"She'll be fine with it." Zac took the envelope and pulled

out the DNA report. "Didn't Cat say that she thought Winnie's sister had meant she'd tell me who the ranch heir was?"

"Yes," Chelsea nodded. "Why?"

"That's not what she meant when she threatened Cat." He turned the DNA report for Chelsea to see. "Look here at the lab technician that worked on the report."

"Dorothy Larson-Conway." Chelsea read the lab tech's name out loud. "Whoa!"

"What?" Zac looked at Chelsea questioningly.

"No wonder Cat thought I knew who Harris's mother was!" Chelsea pointed to the lab tech's name again. "Winnie's sister is Harris's mother!"

"How did I not realize that before?" Zac's eyes widened with realization.

"You weren't thinking about it!" Chelsea said absently. "I was the one who encouraged you to let Dorothy come stay with us. Bessie must've told Cat that."

"You were also the one that vouched for Harris and encouraged me to hire him as the ranch foreman," Zac pointed out. "Didn't you say that he told you he was waiting to meet his aunt that day Cat saw you at Cupids Creek? The day Harris was arrested for trespassing."

"Yes, he did." Chelsea frowned. "Harris is Winnie's nephew and Dorothy's son!"

"Were you two fiddling in my purse?" Cat scared them half to death. She'd come into the room so quietly.

"Sorry, that was me," Zac owned up. "I wanted to see the DNA report again."

"Are we never going to hear the end of this now?" Cat asked, looking pained as she put the tray on the coffee table.

"No, I want my blood retested," Zac told her.

"How are we going to do that?" Cat asked. "Dad is no longer with us."

"I'm sure we must have his DNA all over the place," Zac said hopefully.

"Zac, Dad died thirty-one years ago." Cat shook her head and started to pour coffee for all of them.

"True." Zac sighed. "But we've figured out the lab tech was Winnie's sister."

"Didn't I say that?" Cat asked, handing a cup of coffee to Chelsea and then Zac.

"I don't think so." Chelsea shook her head. "I now know why you thought that I knew who Harris's mother was."

"Ah!" Cat said, sitting back in the armchair with a steaming cup of coffee. "Sorry I accused you."

"I understand." Chelsea smiled. "You obviously knew that Dorothy was Harris's mother?"

"I found that out after I started digging into why my father had doubts about Zac's parentage," Cat told her. "Well, he never doubted Zac was his son. But..." She rolled her eyes, realizing she was getting herself in a twist. "You know what I mean."

"We do!" Chelsea assured her.

"As the second letter was addressed to my mother, I figured it was my mother who'd ordered the DNA test," Cat explained. "So, I called one of my old doctors from the local hospital in Lewistown and he dug into the old records. He found that it was my mom who ordered it. I was shocked when he then asked me if I knew that Winnie's sister was the lab tech who worked on the test."

"Did he give you Dorothy's full name?" Chelsea took a sip of her coffee.

"He did and that is when I put two and two together about Harris." Cat leaned over and took a cookie. "I found out that Winnie was his aunt and Dorothy his mother." She took a bite of the cookie.

"How did they know your mother though?" Chelsea was still a bit vague on that.

"Dorothy, Winnie, and my mother all went to school together," Cat explained. "I called Holly and she confirmed it. They didn't like my mother much. Especially when Dorothy was sort of dating my father when he dropped her for my mother."

"That's right your mom moved to town when she was in high school," Chelsea remembered.

"Actually," Cat said, "my mom lived in Lewistown when she was a little girl."

"Seriously?" Zac looked surprised.

"Yes." Cat nodded. "That's why Holly knew mom from before she moved away."

"So, Harris's mother was also from Lewistown?" Chelsea's eyes narrowed. "You don't think they're somehow mixed up with all this stuff going on with the five ranches?"

"I wouldn't be surprised," Cat said. "From what I can gather the Larson's hated all of us."

"Why?" Chelsea asked.

"I'm not sure, my career started to take off and my investigations hit a dead end." Cat took another sip of her coffee.

"Maybe there would be something in mom's journals or our ancestors' log books," Zac suggested.

"Do you know where all that old stuff from the attic went?" Cat asked Zac.

"No, I've already told you. I have no idea where dad would've moved them to," Zac said, shaking his head.

"Pity." Cat sighed. "I think there are a lot of answers and clues in there."

"Maybe he moved them to the same place he moved his friends' treasures like you said." Zac leaned forward to try to get a cookie. Chelsea picked one up and gave it to him.

"Do you know who that friend was?" Chelsea took a cookie for herself. "Because maybe they would know where your father took everything to."

"It was my grandfather." David's voice made them all jump, and their heads turned towards where he was leaning casually against the door frame. "Sorry, didn't mean to make you jump. I knocked but no one answered, and Janine told me you were all here."

"Your grandfather?" Zac's brows creased together.

"Yes," David confirmed. "May I?" He took his hat off and pointed to an armchair.

'Yes, of course, come in," Zac invited him.

"Can I get you a cup of coffee?" Cat offered, her eyes narrowing suspiciously at David.

"Please," David accepted the offer.

"Before you sit down, could I have a word with you in private about that other matter we were discussing earlier," Cat said through gritted teeth.

"Excuse me," David said to Zac. Chelsea followed and obviously annoyed Cat into the kitchen.

"What do you think that's all about?" Zac asked Chelsea.

"I'm not sure but Cat looked pretty irritated." Chelsea looked towards the kitchen. "Want me to eavesdrop?" She grinned.

"Do you think we should?" Zac didn't look convinced. "Let's rather put them both on the spot when they come back."

"Ooh, vicious. But I like it." Chelsea laughed.

"In the meantime, you can tell me what you need my help with." Zac took a bite of his cookie, eyeing her out curiously as he wondered what she was going to say.

Chapter Ten

THE PLAN TO SAVE MOUNTAIN RISE RANCH

Cat stormed into the kitchen and swirled around to glare at David.

"What are you doing here?" Cat hissed.

"I came to find you," David told her. "I heard you chatting, so I waited politely until there was a gap to announce my presence."

"You know what they say about eavesdropping!" Cat warned him.

"Come now, Cat." David looked around the kitchen. "Nice place you have here."

"You need to go!" Cat told him.

"You offered me coffee," David reminded her. "I would really love a cup."

"You can be so insufferable!" Cat marched over to a cupboard and pulled out another cup. "One cup and then you go!"

"And miss out on all the fun?" David took the coffee cup Cat shoved at him.

"One cup and then go!" Cat started to storm out of the kitchen.

"Or we could talk to Chelsea and Zac together," David suggested. "You know about our plan?"

"Now is not a good time for our plan!" Cat turned around

and walked into her brother. "Zac!"

"What plan do you and David want to talk to me and Chelsea about?" Zac asked her.

"Is that why you came to my house that day?" Chelsea popped her head around Zac.

"Let's all go take a seat and we can continue this conversation over a cup of coffee," David said. "I've been out in the fields for hours and I could really use a cup."

"Sure." Zac turned and hobbled back into the living room.

David followed Zac out of the kitchen while Chelsea stayed behind.

"Please don't be mad at me," Cat said to Chelsea. "But David and I wanted to help you get Mountain Rise out of trouble."

"How do you know that Mountain Rise is in trouble?" Chelsea's eyes narrowed. "Did one of my kids say something?"

"No." Cat shook her head. "Your mother did."

"Excuse me?" Chelsea's brows furrowed. "My mother?"

"She wrote to me about five months ago." Cat pointed towards the living room. "I have her letter with me in my purse."

"Is your Mary Poppins purse filled with mystery letters?" Chelsea asked Cat. "Do you just keep yanking out a bottomless amount of letters?"

They stood staring at each for a few seconds then burst out laughing at the absurdity of everything going on around them.

"I'm sorry," Cat said, wiping her eyes and holding her belly. "But that was a great reference."

"I know, I do come up with them now and then." Chelsea leaned back against the counter. "I'm sorry I didn't mean to get upset. I know you only want to help, and I appreciate it. Normally I'd stiffen up and get all huffy around now, but I also admit when I'm in trouble."

"No, you don't," Cat said. "I can remember quite a few times you've been in trouble and didn't reach out. I had to help you from a distance anonymously."

"What are you talking about?" Chelsea's eyes narrowed once again.

"I have all the letters in my Mary Poppins postal bag!" Cat grinned.

"My mother!" Chelsea threw up her hands in exasperation. "You were her mystery aunt that lived across the country!"

"Guilty," Cat admitted.

Chelsea stood staring at Cat for a few seconds. Cat was getting a little nervous hoping she hadn't offended Chelsea as she was enjoying the thought of being friends again. But then Chelsea did something to surprise Cat. She pulled Cat to her for a huge hug.

"Thank you so much, mysterious Aunt, from across the country." Chelsea sighed. "You saved the ranch more than once over the past few years that my mother's been ill."

"You know no matter what, Chels, I'd always have your back!" Cat told her.

"I think deep down I always knew it was you." Chelsea shook her head and stepped back.

"Your mother did say once or twice that she thought you suspected as much." Cat pointed to the door. "I think we'd better go join the men."

"Is there something between you and David?" Chelsea stopped Cat from leaving the kitchen. "David's a good guy, Cat. But I've always felt there is something secretive about him. So please be careful."

"Don't worry, there is nothing between us," Cat assured Chelsea. "We're just joining forces to get to the bottom of what is going on with all the trouble around here."

"Okay." Chelsea nodded. "Now let's go hear this plan of yours."

Cat followed Chelsea into the living room.

"*L*et me get this straight," Chelsea looked at Cat and then Zac. "Cat wants to invest in the Mountain Rise and turn it into an Inn following the Cupids Bow Inn model."

"Yes," Cat confirmed.

"Then Zac and David want to invest in setting up a breeding stable, following the Cupids Bow Stables?" Chelsea's eyes narrowed as she looked at Zac. "But I keep full ownership of the ranch?"

"Correct," David said. "We only want to invest in the inn and stables."

"Your land stays your land, and you get full control of decorations, renovations, staffing, and the running of your ranch," Cat told her. "We're just silent investors."

"But you'll all help me get it set up and started?" Chelsea bit her bottom lip in contemplation.

"As investors, one of our first priorities is to bring you and Mountain Rise out of the red." Cat sat back.

Chelsea looked at the proposal Cat had pulled out of her magic purse. She couldn't believe what she was seeing. Chelsea had to swallow down the lump in her throat and she knew her eyes must be all watery. But she couldn't help it. When she came here today, she felt like she had come looking for a handout. Chelsea had spent the entire previous evening swallowing her pride, knowing she had to do something or lose her home. There was no way she was going to let her kids dip into their trust funds to bail her out. So today she'd sucked up the last bit of pride, straightened her shoulders, held her head high, and drove over to her ex-husband's ranch to ask him for his help. After all, he had offered a few months ago but Chelsea hadn't really been in a state to listen to him.

To be honest she was a little angry at him as he was also seeing someone. Chelsea had known that was irrational. She had no right to be jealous or angry about who Zac dated. They'd been divorced for fourteen years. But each time she saw him with someone else it killed her a little more. She felt like he was slicing out another piece of her heart with a hot knife and draining her soul. Chelsea kept telling herself that was being ridiculous. It was her choice to leave and not try to save their marriage. Yes, Zac had kissed another woman and she'd known he'd been attracted to her. But he'd never acted on that attraction and the woman had thrown herself at him right at the moment she knew Chelsea would see.

When Chelsea had questioned Zac about it, he'd been nothing but honest with her. Right down to admitting he found the woman attractive, but he'd never jeopardize their marriage. Chelsea was the light that lit his heart, his soul, and his life. Without her, Zac said he felt like he'd be living in perpetual darkness. She was as important to him as the air he breathed and every day he fell deeper in love with her. Chelsea had always loved his use of words. Some might say they were cheesy, but she loved them. Zac had always made her feel like his queen. Never did he ever make her feel like she was anything less than a full partner in their marriage, their business, and their lives.

But after that incident with that woman who was after him and making no effort to hide the fact, Chelsea felt her trust in him slipping. When he went to a vet conference, she'd spend the time wondering if that other vet who was after him was there. Zac was an incredibly handsome man, and he caught the eye of every woman regardless of their relationship status. Some didn't even care about his. The more unavailable Zac was to these women the more they went after him. Eventually, Chelsea didn't recognize herself. She'd become a jealous untrusting person which she'd never been, and she didn't like herself. That's when she realized how unhappy she was and how trapped she started to feel in her marriage.

Eventually, Chelsea got to a stage where she couldn't stand to be near Zac. When he tried to be affectionate with her, she'd pull away and start a fight. Soon they were fighting nearly every day until Zac couldn't take it anymore. He wanted them to go to marriage counseling and work through what was going on between them. But Chelsea was willing to. That's when Harris had caught her eye. Of course, she never did anything with Harris while she and Zac were still married. Chelsea had gone on her first date with Harris only two months after her divorce with

Zac was finalized. That had been the worst mistake of her life. At first, Harris was charming and attentive. But she soon realized he wasn't Zac.

After four dates Chelsea had broken it off with Harris because they weren't working out. That's when Harris once again showed the same colors he'd done beneath the bleachers when they were at high school, and he'd attack Cat's character. None of her family knew about it but Chelsea had to eventually get a restraining order. She had to lie to her family and tell them she'd lost her phone to get a new number. But her family started to notice a change in her. She was moody, jumpy, and on edge all the time Chelsea started to live in fear that Harris would go after and harass her children.

When Cat had thought that Harris was the one who'd hurt Callum all those years ago Chelsea's first thought was that she had a feeling he was quite capable of it. The only two people in the world he seemed to care about were his aunt and mother. Although he never told her who his mother or aunt were. Harris only ever referred to them as his mother and aunt. His father had died in a mountain climbing accident when he was sixteen and that's why he and his mother moved back to Lewistown. They moved into a beautifully restored old house in Lewistown owned by his mother's uncle. He'd shown Chelsea the house on one of their dinner dates. She was sure the house had once belonged to old Mr. Watson who owned the Farm Store and Auction House. But Chelsea hadn't said anything because it wasn't really any of her business.

Chelsea frowned as a thought ran through her mind. Were Harris, Winnie, and Dorothy related to old Mr. Watson? If he was Winnie's and Dorothy's uncle, he could've been their mother's brother. That led Chelsea to wonder if the Watsons had ever had anything against any of the five families on farms surrounding hers. Or maybe Mr. Watson could tell them something about it. Although Chelsea had heard he was very ill, and that his son had taken over his business. None of them knew Mr. Watson's only son as he'd gone to some snooty private boarding school as he was some kind of genius or something. Chelsea couldn't ever remember meeting the guy either and wondered if Zac had ever met him.

"Chelsea?" Cat snapped her fingers in the air. "Hey, you got your glazed daydreaming look about you."

"Oh, sorry," Chelsea snapped back to the present. "You said you and David wanted to find out where the trouble started as well as why."

"We do," David confirmed.

"Cat!" Zac looked at her with big, worried eyes. "I don't want you getting involved in that. You've already been shot at." He looked at David. "You were shot."

"All the more reason I want to get to the bottom of this," Cat told Zac. "If you try to stop me, I'll just investigate behind your back."

"You're doing that already!" Zac pointed out.

"We were going to tell you as soon as we'd spoken to Chelsea about a plan to help the ranch," David told Zac.

"Oh!" Zac pulled an oops face. "Sorry, I didn't mean to jump the gun on that."

"It's okay," Cat said. "I understand."

"I have a confession to make," David cleared his throat. "I heard a lot more of the conversation today than I let on."

"I know!" Zac told him. "I wanted you to hear it."

"I don't understand why you would." David's brow furrowed and he looked at Zac suspiciously.

"Because, David, like it or not you're a part of our family," Zac told him. "Your father married the woman who was our second mother."

"I know," David said.

"Today is a day that we drop all our secrets." Zac's eyes narrowed. "I know you've been keeping a lot of them."

"I..." David's eyes immediately traveled to Cat.

"Don't look at me, we had a deal, remember?" Cat told him.

"What deal?" Chelsea looked at Cat.

"Oh, it's just something between myself and David." Cat smiled.

"Cat didn't tell me anything," Zac assured David. "Although now I'm a bit hurt that she didn't come to me if she knew what they were."

"Not my secrets to tell!" Cat shrugged.

"Your brother told me." Zac gave David a smug smile when his eyes widened.

"You know David's brother?" Cat's eyes were just as big with surprise as David's were.

"I do," Zac told them. "I've known for years. After all, he did save my life when I was shot."

"Wallace Black?" Chelsea choked. "He's David's brother?"

"Yes," Cat nodded. "My bodyguard is David's older half-brother."

"Do you have different fathers?" Chelsea asked him.

"No, different mothers," David told Chelsea. "Wallace goes by Black as his professional name. His agency got it changed professionally and redacted his true identity."

"Oh!" It was Chelsea's turn to get wide-eyed with surprise.

"He wanted to protect his family due to the nature of his chosen profession," David explained. "We don't usually speak about it. Wallace and I also haven't been on the best of terms in years."

"And why is that?" Zac folded his arms across his chest and looked at David chillingly.

"Why do I get the feeling you already know?" David eyed Zac suspiciously.

"Am I missing something here?" Chelsea asked, feeling a little left out of the loop.

"While Cat and David were laying out their proposal to you, didn't you wonder how a ranch foreman could afford such an outlay to invest in the horse stables he proposed?" Zac asked Chelsea.

"Now that you pointed it out, I am," Chelsea told Zac and

looked at David for an explanation. "But his father did own a horse ranch that he sold."

"Yes, but do you think it would've given David the type of capital he's proposing to outlay not only for your ranch but mine and the three others?" Zac raised his eyebrows as he looked at her.

"If he invested the money and made good on those investments, maybe?" Chelsea shrugged.

"Too short of a period for that," Zac pointed out.

"Okay I don't want to play twenty questions here," Chelsea started to get irritated with this game Zac was playing and his toying with David who was looking uncomfortable.

"Tell us, David," Zac challenged him once again.

"All right!" David cracked under Zac's scrutiny. "I owned a large development and construction company."

"Why are you a foreman if you own a development company?" Chelsea looked at him in amazement. Then something dawned on her. "Wait, what development company?"

An image of the offers for her land from a development company she'd been getting year after year for the past fifteen years flashed through her mind.

"Well?" Zac looked at David. "Answer Chelsea."

"Why are you doing this Zac?" David asked him. "I've been nothing but loyal to you, the land. I have tried to help get to the bottom of all the trouble that has been plaguing the area for years." A shadow crossed his eyes. "I've worked hard day and night to help you get this place into shape."

"What development company, David?" Chelsea said more forcefully

A bad feeling started to claw at the pit of her stomach. Silently she hoped it wasn't the one that had plagued her mother and her for all these years.

"Donaldson's Construction," David said softly and looked Chelsea directly in the eye.

"How did you come to own Donaldson's construction?" Chelsea pushed him to answer her question.

"Old man Donaldson was my grandfather," David admitted.

"You're related to Ron Hicks?" Chelsea hissed.

"He's my cousin on my late mother's side," David explained to Chelsea. "I never knew my mother or her side of the family. My father kept me far away from them as he didn't like them." A muscle at the side of his jaw ticked. "One day my grandfather approached me when I was in my final year at high school."

"Do you mind?" Cat smiled when she saw he was struggling to reveal his family history because he was such a private person. "David at first rejected his grandfather and went home to tell his father. His father then met with old man Donaldson and David's father let him meet the man."

"I was never interested in development or construction. All I ever wanted to do was run a ranch and breed horses," David admitted. "But once I'd finished college and left the military I was lost. My father wanted to sell the farm and I didn't have the money to buy it."

"So, you started working for your grandfather," Chelsea guessed.

"Yes," David nodded. "To my surprise, I was good at the job and turned his construction company into the empire it was before I sold it."

"Why are you even here, David?" Chelsea asked him. "How do we know it's not you behind all this trouble. Because I, Four Lakes, Double A, Big Valley, and Cupids Bow have all been plagued by your development company for years to sell our land."

"That wasn't me nor was it my company," David told her. "My grandfather broke away from Donaldson's Development Corporation. He bought out the construction site and that's the side of the business I took over."

"But you are still associated with the development company," Chelsea pointed out. "I thought for a moment a little while ago that maybe all these problems were caused by Harris's family."

"Harris Conway?" David frowned.

"Yes." Chelsea nodded.

Before Chelsea could stop herself, she blurted out the whole story of the hell Harris put her through when she broke things off with him. She told them about the restraining order and how he had stalked her. The rumors and lies Harris spread about her like they were engaged. That he caught her cheating and ended things. Meanwhile, he wasn't allowed within a few feet of her.

"Chelsea, why didn't you come to me?" Zac looked at her. His eyes filled with worry.

"It was my mess." Chelsea gave him a small smile. "I couldn't come running back to you every time I had a problem."

"Chelsea." Zac took her hand. "You know how I feel. I think I've made that quite clear over the years. I am always here for you."

"I know." Chelsea's eyes misted over. "But I hurt you and was so mean to you."

"You were going through something." Zac kissed the top of her hand affectionately. "I just wish you had let me in and not locked me out. I would've given you your space. Heck, I would've pulled every star out of the sky for you if you wanted it."

"Uh..." Cat drew their attention to her.

Chelsea had almost forgotten that David and Cat were in the room with them.

"David and I have a thing," Cat sat then glanced at David who nodded and stood up.

"Oh, yes, we do and..." David made a show of looking at his wristwatch. "We're late for the thing." He reached down and picked up his hat.

Cat stood and picked up her purse. "Let's meet tomorrow at Mountain Rise to go over everything."

"And maybe David can continue his story?" Zac wasn't letting David off the hook.

"Sure," David promised as she ushered Cat out of the living and then out of the house.

"Lock up when you leave," Cat called from the front door.

"That was getting a little awkward and uncomfortable," Cat said as she and David walked towards the stables.

"I'll say," David agreed. "I'm sorry, I thought you were the one to tell Zac about me."

"Nope, it wasn't me," Cat assured him. "But I have something to ask you."

"Okay," David said, his eyes narrowing.

"I've learned that you were in the office of the arena the day of my father's accident," Cat told him.

"Ah." David nodded. "Chelsea and Zac told you."

"Yes," Cat confirmed. "Did you see anyone during the time you were staying there arguing with my father?"

"No, I snuck in and out when there was no one around," David told her. "Why?"

"Because Chelsea thought she saw Ron Hicks arguing with my father right before his accident," Cat explained. "She was in the office getting your things."

"Ron?" David asked her, looking surprised. "I don't think it was Ron."

"Why?" Cat asked him.

"Because he'd been working in Texas on a training construction crew," David told her. "Wallace was trying to find out who'd framed me for a crime I didn't commit."

"Yes, I know about that too," Cat said.

"Wallace thought it might have been Ron who framed me, but he was nowhere near Montana at the time." David looked thoughtful for a while. "It could've been his father, though."

"His father?" Cat looked at David.

"Yes, he also worked for Donaldson's Development." David opened the passenger door to his pickup for her. "I think he might've been at old man Donaldson's place around then. He was looking for my grandfather's treasures."

"Seriously?" Cat's eyes widened. "He was the henchman your great grandfather sent to find it?"

"Yes, although thug is more the word I'd use." David closed the passenger door once Cat was in and walked around to the driver's side.

"Do you know if they may have had a problem with my father?" Cat put the seatbelt on.

"I've been investigating that for many years, Cat," David shocked her by saying.

"Excuse me?" Cat's eyes widened.

"Your father was a great man, Cat." David started the car and backed out of his parking space. "He knew I was living in the stables. He made sure I was warm, he brought in a cot for me, and would bring me food every night."

"Then why were you sneaking around?" Cat asked him.

"I was wanted," David told her. "Your father told me that he'd take me in a heartbeat, but he was worried about Winnie."

"Ah-ha, I knew it!" Cat snapped her fingers. "I knew my father was having reservations about her."

"It was more than that," David said. "He'd asked my brother to help him investigate her and her family for some reason."

"Did Wallace tell you what that reason was?" Cat asked him.

"No," David told her honestly. "All they would tell me was that it was better if I didn't know. Especially as I was in so much trouble already."

"That sounds like something both my father and your brother would do." Cat sighed. "So, we still don't know why he'd started divorce proceedings, and now you tell me he was investigating her."

"Not necessarily." David grinned. "We've still got Wallace."

"We do!" Cat's face lit up with excitement. "But I know he's been well trained, so how the heck are we supposed to squeeze information out of him?"

"I know a way, but you're probably not going to like it," David told her.

"Try me," Cat challenged, then looked around her. "Where are we going?"

"Oh, to find that magic elf," David once again surprised her by saying.

"So, you did hear all of that?" Cat accused him.

"I already knew," David shrugged.

"Wait a minute." Cat's eyes narrowed suspiciously as she stared at him. "How do you know who the magic elf is?"

"Your father and I had long chats when he came to sneak me food," David told her. "Two days before his accident he came to me and asked me to do him a favor."

"Let me guess, he told you about Zac and then bestowed some sacred quest on you!" Cat teased him.

"Actually, that was pretty accurate." David laughed. "He told me that Zac would one day find out some news that you would deliver to him. He told me it had to do with some medical documents. That's when he made me promise to look out for the both of you."

"My father asked you to look out for us, why?" Cat was amazed. "He hardly knew you."

"I met your father many times Cat," David assured her. "He often came to visit my father. They were good friends."

"Why am I only learning about this now?" Cat asked him.

"I don't know," David said. "When the envelope was eventually opened, I was to take you to the person who you've named the magic elf."

"That's what you were looking for in my purse?" Cat said.

"Oh, you did see that?" David's cheeks reddened. "I'm sorry. But yes, I've been hunting for that letter for a while now. I needed to know if you'd opened it or not."

"Well, I've had it with me all these years," Cat told him. "So, you wouldn't have found it in my room at the house, Zac's house, or my new house."

"Oh, you saw me snooping around there as well?" He looked at her. "I'm so sorry."

"At least I know you weren't trying to sabotage us now," Cat said.

"Is that what you thought?" David looked at her amazed.

"Oh, another thing." Cat turned in her seat to look at him. "I believe you speak French."

"Yes, why?" David glanced at her.

"How much of the conversation did you hear between my father and I in the arena the day of his accident?" Cat asked him.

"Oh, that!" David nodded and glanced out the other side window. "Would you believe me if I said I heard nothing?"

"No!" Cat shook her head. "Try again."

"Okay, I heard most of it," David admitted.

"Who have you told?" She raised her eyebrows.

"No one," David assured her. "I'm not a snitch, Cat." He raised an eyebrow and smiled. "Mm, it seems now I'm the one who knows your secret."

"Don't push your luck," Cat told him. "I still have that last secret, remember?"

"Unbelievable," David sighed and shook his head.

"So, I think we're even," Cat gave him a smug smile.

"Fine," David admitted grudgingly. "But we're still partners in this, right?"

"Of course. I think we're in too deep for either of us to back out now," Cat assured him.

"Good," David pulled into the Halls ranch.

"Why are we going to..." Cat suddenly realized who the magic elf was. "Ashley's the magic elf?"

"Yup," David nodded. "She's also the one I've been working with all these years trying to figure out who is responsible for all the trouble on the land."

"Ashley?" Cat frowned. "My best friend, Ashley?"

"Ashley and her husband, Billy," David corrected her. "She's the reason I've also been searching for that letter. It's been driving her nuts to find out what was in it."

"Oh, I'm pretty sure she knows," Cat told him. "She's a rather smart magic elf."

Chapter Eleven

MEET THE TRUE MARSHALL MYERS

It had been two weeks since Chelsea had gone to Cupids Bow Ranch to ask Zac for help. Since then, Cat and David had been to Mountain Rise nearly every day. They'd been sorting through plans and ideas to turn Mountain Rise into an inn like Cupids Bow was. David was helping Chelsea with the stables and their cost, which included new horses.

Chelsea looked in her bedroom mirror one more time. She couldn't believe how nervous she was feeling because Zac was coming over to help in twenty minutes. He no longer had a cast on, and Cat had told her he'd even moved back into his room upstairs.

"Get a grip, Chelsea," she said to her reflection. "You've been to see him nearly every second day over the past two weeks."

And every second day here I'd be standing and faffing with my appearance like a sixteen-year-old with her first crush. Well, Zac was her first crush. She laughed and shook her head.

"I've been speaking to my own reflection for too long," Chelsea gave her hair one more quick brush. "Wandering around in the big old house on my own has finally made me lose my mind."

She smoothed her soft, flowing, blue cotton shirt down once more before forcing herself to leave her room. Zac would probably never give her a second chance. Chelsea had hurt him and could never expect him to just forget about that. When she reached the top of the stairs the doorbell rang, and Chelsea's heart went wild. She even felt her hands begin to shake and impulsively ran her hands through her hair.

"I'll get it, Daphne," Chelsea called to her housekeeper.

Chelsea made a mental note to remind herself to speak to Zac about helping her with Daphne's retirement fund. She'd told Chelsea that she would never just leave her, but she did want to retire soon. Chelsea sighed.

"Where on earth will ever find another Daphne?" She said, walking towards the front door.

Chelsea pulled it open, and her heart went all kinds of crazy when she saw Zac standing there without his crutches. He looked so handsome with a big grin on his face. He held up a large brown paper bag with her favorite restaurant's logo on it.

"I brought us all a brunch," Zac said.

"Well, then you are most definitely welcome," Chelsea teased, stepping back to let him in. "How does it feel to not be using crutches?"

"I feel like I've just been let out of solitary confinement," Zac told her, dipping down and kissing her on the head.

He'd always done that when they met, even after their divorce, so she had no idea why her heart went a little crazier than it already was. Zac walked into the house and headed straight for the kitchen. That's when Chelsea spotted the pie he's hidden behind his back.

"Is that a peach pie for Daphne?" Chelsea asked him, smiling.

"Yes, from Dove bakery," Zac confirmed.

"You know you've never had to bribe Daphne to like you because she always had a soft spot for you," Chelsea pointed.

"That's because he always brings me my favorite peach pie," Daphne popped out of the kitchen, walked up to Zac, and gave him a kiss on the cheek. "You look a lot better, young man."

"Thank you, Daphne, I feel like a new man." He gave her the

big brown bag. "I brought you your favorite dish from the diner too," he whispered.

"If only I was younger." Daphne gave an exaggerated sigh. "Now, hand over the pie!"

"Of course." Zac pulled the pie from behind his back and gave it to her. "I got you extra-large this time. Holly told me you can freeze it."

"She didn't happen to slip the recipe for her pie?" Daphne looked at him hopefully.

"You know she'll never part with those recipes," Chelsea told her. "I think she's going to take it with her to the grave."

"I think her secret ingredient is fresh basil," Zac whispered again.

"That might just be the taste I miss when I try to copy the recipe." Daphne looked up at Zack wide-eyed.

"Wow!" Chelsea said, impressed. "How did you get that out of Holly?"

"She told me to tell Daphne," Zac admitted.

"Thank you, Zac," Daphne said. "I'll go put these in the kitchen." She looked up at him. "Would you like something to drink or eat?"

"Not right now, thank you, Daphne." Zac patted his rock hard abs that his t-shirt outlined. "I've already had two cups of coffee. One at the restaurant when I went to get the food and one with Holly at the bakery."

"I bet you had a cinnamon bun as well at the bakery!" Chelsea raised her eyebrows.

"Guilty!" Zac laughed. "I had to have one. When I was confined, I wasn't allowed any confectionery contraband."

"Give me a holler when you want something." Daphne turned and walked into the kitchen.

"I thought we could sit in the study," Chelsea told him.

"Would you mind if we go around the stables and immediate surroundings?" Zac asked her. "I don't feel like being cooped up in a study just yet."

"Sure, I'll get the plans I've been working on with Cat and David," Chelsea ducked into the office and picked up the folder.

"I've always loved this study," Zac said from the doorway, making her jump by how silently he'd crept up.

"It's the one place I've asked not to be changed," Chelsea told him.

"I don't blame you." Zac looked around. "There's too much history and many memories between these four walls."

"Yes, there is," Chelsea agreed, and her heart suddenly felt heavy.

"Chels, you don't have to turn your home into an inn if you don't want to," Zac walked into the study and stood in front of her. "We can find another way."

Chelsea could feel his body heat and smell his familiar cologne. She had to stop herself from reaching up and putting her arms around him like she used to do when they were married and she needed comfort.

"No, I'm quite excited about this venture." Chelsea handed Zac the file. "I've spoken to the kids, and they too are excited about it. I think Hayden's said something along the lines of becoming a land baron one day with two prosperous horse ranches while Jamie wants to own both of the inns."

"Nice to know our children are already planning out their inheritances." Zac laughed. "Aren't they going to be surprised when we both live to well over a hundred?"

"Let's hope it's not that long," Chelsea said. "Unless science has found a way to keep us from physically showing signs of age."

"I agree that we don't want to live that long in an old body." Zac grinned.

Their eyes locked and their words faded away with the world around them. Chelsea felt like the invisible thread that had once bound them was still there pulling her toward him. Zac's lips started to move toward hers but before they could meet, the doorbell chimed, making them jump apart.

"I'll get it," Chelsea called and nearly knocked Zac flying when she rushed out of the room.

Her body felt like it was vibrating, and her heart was doing its wild dance inside her chest once again. By the time Chelsea got to the door, she had admitted to herself that was still very much in love with her ex-husband and always had been.

"Hello," Chelsea's voice was a pitch too high as she greeted Cat and David. "I wasn't expecting you today."

"Mm," was all Cat said, her eyes narrowing suspiciously making Chelsea's cheeks heat up with guilt.

"Hi, sorry we thought we'd join you and Zac to collate everything we've done so far." David gave Cat a peculiar look.

"That's an excellent idea." Chelsea's voice was still at a pitch she didn't recognize.

Her eyes met Cat's, who shot up one eyebrow. A slow smile spread across her lips. Cat suspected something! It was Chelsea's fault for not being able to control her wayward emotions and pounding heart.

"Come in," Chelsea stepped aside and let them in.

"Can I have a word with you in private, please?" Cat asked Chelsea. "We have that thing we need to discuss."

"Uh..." Chelsea's eyes darted to David who shrugged and frowned. "Sure." She knew if she didn't go with Cat now, she'd be the constant object of Cat's knowing looks. "Zac is in the study." She told David and led Cat upstairs to her bedroom.

When they got to the bedroom Cat grabbed Chelsea's wrist, pulled her into the room, and closed the door.

"Okay, out with it!" Cat leaned against the door and folded her arms across her chest. "What has got you all breathless and hyped?"

"Nothing," Chelsea lied. "I'm just so excited about our plans."

"Uh-huh," Cat said, not believing a word of what Chelsea had just said. "Can I tell you what I think is happening?"

"Don't you think we should go back downstairs to go over everything?" Chelsea said.

"No." Cat shook her head. "No more secrets, remember?"

"Oh, but aren't you still carrying some?" Chelsea pointed out.

"I'll make you a deal." Cat raised an eyebrow once again. "I'll come over later with a bottle of wine, spend the night, and I'll tell you everything you want to know."

"Seriously?" Chelsea asked with a smile. "I would love that."

"Then we have a deal?" Cat asked her.

"Deal." Chelsea held her hand out. "But don't get any of that cheap chardonnay."

"Chels, I haven't drunk that stuff since we sneaked a few glasses at my father's wedding," Cat told her.

"Great, because it gives me such a headache," Chelsea told her.

"I think that stuff is enough to burn your insides," Cat said. "Now out with it!"

"It's nothing," Chelsea assured Cat. "A stupid mistake that I can't fix."

"If you're talking about my brother," Cat looked Chelsea in the eye, "then you have to tell him how you feel about him because he's not going to make the first move again."

"I don't think I can do that," Chelsea admitted. "I wouldn't know how to do that."

"Just tell him the truth," Cat suggested.

"I'd die if he didn't feel the same way or turned me down." Chelsea swallowed and wrung her hands nervously.

"I can't vouch for how Zac will react," Cat told her honestly. "But I do know by the way he looks at you that he still loves you."

"I don't know." Chelsea shook her head. "I think I'll just see how things go over the next few months because we're going to be working closely together."

"Life's too short to wait for tomorrow, Chels," Cat warned her. "There's no time like the present." She smiled, spun around, and walked out of Chelsea's room leaving her standing there staring after Cat.

"What are you doing?" Chelsea ran after Cat.

"Nothing," Cat looked back at her. "I'm going to look over everything we've discussed and go through the to-do lists."

"Okay." Chelsea breathed a sigh of relief. For a moment, she could've sworn she saw that mischievous look in Cat's eyes that usually meant she was up to something.

"There you are," Zac greeted Cat. "Where did you go off to?"

"I needed some lip balm," Cat lied. "Chels, do you mind if I ask Daphne to make me a cup of coffee?"

"Of course, go ahead." Chelsea took a seat next to Zac on the sofa that was in the office to look at the file.

"I see Daphne is still possessive over her kitchen." David laughed.

"Yes, we're not even allowed to make a cup of coffee." Chelsea shook her head.

"That's because there's a place for everything and Daphne loves everything to be in its place." Zac smiled and leaned forward to look over the architectural drawings, Indy, had done for Chelsea. "My nephew is very talented."

"That he is," Chelsea agreed. "I love how he's managed to incorporate the old style of the stables with the upgrade."

"Indy doesn't like destroying historical structures," Zac told them. "He'd rather find a way to merge the old and new."

"I love it." Chelsea ran her fingers over the design following the rooms, stalls, and even an indoor arena like Cupids Bow. "He's even put in a veterinary room."

"Yes, it's much easier for us vets to come to the ranch, and it helps if you're set up correctly," Zac told her. "The room will work for livestock and wild animals too, not only horses."

"It's awesome, Zac." Chelsea breathed. "We must still discuss the barbeque this Saturday for the five ranches to get them on board with the plans and discuss strategy."

"I've already gotten word to Four Lakes. Ryan is actually going to venture out of hiding to attend," Zac surprised them by saying. "Cat spoke to Maria and Brett from Big Valley."

"I went over to Double A yesterday and spoke to Greg Watson. Tammy Anderson wasn't there," David told them. "Greg said he'd get word to Tammy."

"Do you have Tammy Anderson's number?" Chelsea asked David.

"I have her number," David said, reaching into his pocket and pulling out a piece of paper with a number on it which he handed to Chelsea.

"I'll give her a call," Chelsea promised.

"Thank you," Zac smiled at Chelsea. "We need her support because Gregg is not the one who owns Double A."

"I'll tell her that." Chelsea made a mental note to contact Tammy before Cat came around later that evening.

"David," Cat said, walking into the study. She had hers and David's coats in her hand. "Can we please take Daphne into Lewistown? She needs some supplies."

"I can take her tomorrow," Chelsea started to stand up, but Cat stopped her.

"No, not necessary. I saw your takeout. Now David and I are dying for some of that." Cat shoved David's coat into his hands. "Come along, Daphne is waiting for us at your pick-up."

Chelsea suddenly realized what Cat was doing. *Sneaky!* Her eyes narrowed as they met Cat's but all she did was give Chelsea an innocent smile in return.

"We won't be long." Cat looked at her wristwatch. "It'll probably only take about an hour or two."

"Okay, in the meantime, Chelsea and I will go around the stables," Zac told them.

"Good!" Cat nodded, pushing David out the door. "We'll be back soon."

Chelsea sat staring at the empty door in amazement and suddenly feeling exposed.

"On the bright side..." Chelsea tried to make light conversation. "We can now make coffee without Daphne's eagle eyeing us in case we make a mess or put something in a different place."

"I like the sound of that," Zac told her. "Let's go. I'll help with the coffee and fish out where Daphne hides the cookies."

"Oh, I can show you that," Chelsea promised, standing up and following Zac from the study.

Zac and Chelsea worked in unison as they put the coffee pot on, and grabbed some cups, the cream, and sugar. They both reached for the honey at the same time, and their hands touched. Instead of Zac pulling away, he folded Chelsea's hand into his and turned her towards them. Their eyes locked once again. Words were suddenly no longer necessary as their lips moved towards each other. Chelsea's breath caught in her throat and her eyes drifted shut as they melted into a kiss.

The doorbell rang once again, making the jump apart. They stood staring at each in shock for a few seconds before the doorbell chimed again. Chelsea turned and walked to the front of the house on shaky legs with Zac following close behind her. She pulled the door open and found Maria Parker standing there with a tall, good looking man.

"Hi, Chelsea," Maria greeted her. "This is West Lockran, Cat's manager."

"Hi." Chelsea greeted them both.

"Janine at Cupids Bow told us Cat was here," Maria explained. "I hope you don't mind us dropping in like this, but West needs to speak with Cat urgently."

"Hello, Maria," Zac stepped around Chelsea and then shook hands with West. "Hi, Cat told me you'd be coming to Montana. I think she was expecting you two weeks ago."

"Circumstance arose," West told him.

"Ah, I take it by circumstance you mean Paul's vacation to Cupids Bow?" Zac grinned.

"Something like that." West nodded. "Is Cat here?"

"Cat, David, and my housekeeper have gone into Lewistown

to get some supplies," Chelsea told them. "We're just making some coffee if you'd like to come in and wait for her?"

"Thank you," West accepted the invitation and practically pushed Maria through the front door.

"Do you mind if I take our horses to your paddock?" Maria asked Chelsea.

"Not at all," Chelsea said. "Zac can finish making the coffee and I'll help you."

"Or Zac and I can see to the horses," West offered.

"No, we'll be just fine," Chelsea declined his offer.

Zac led the way to the kitchen with West following him.

"Zac, is Wallace with Cat?" West asked him when they were in the kitchen.

"No, he is at Cupids Bow going over security with my inn manager, why?" Zac frowned. He didn't like the look of worry that bordered on dread in West's eyes.

"Do you have a car here?" West asked Zac.

"Yes, my pickup's out front," Zac told him, and fear started to grip him. "What's going on, West?"

"I'll explain along the way," West assured him. "We have to go find Cat. You need to call Wallace along the way and advise him of whatever other routes they could be taking into Lewistown."

"Okay, now you're scaring me," Zac said, immediately starting to walk out of the kitchen to get his keys, coat, and hat.

"I'm scared too," West told him. "But we can discuss this along the way."

"Along the way to where?" Chelsea and Maria suddenly appeared behind them.

"We're going to find Cat," Zac explained.

"Why?" Chelsea and Maria said together then looked at each other.

"You never did tell me why you needed to find Cat so urgently," Maria pointed out.

"No time to stand here talking," West turned and started walking towards the front door. "I'll explain along the way."

"That's what you promised me you'd do when we left Big Valley Ranch," Maria reminded him.

The four of them piled into Zac's twin cab pickup. Zac handed Chelsea his phone.

"Can you please call Wallace and let him know we need to help us find Cat?" Zac asked her. The adrenaline from fear and shock was starting to course through his veins. "When you've told him, give the phone to West so he can explain to all of us at once what is going on."

Chelsea nodded and dialed Wallace's number as Zac sped out of the ranch's drive onto the road that would link them with the main route to Lewistown. She explained to Wallace what was going on but before she could hand the phone over to West another call came in.

"It's Cat!" Chelsea said and hit the answer button.

"Why are you doing this, Marshall?" Cat sounded angry on the other end.

Chelsea and Maria looked at each wide-eyed before Maria leaned over and pressed the mute button.

"I think she wants us to hear this," Maria told them, glancing at Zac in the mirror.

Chelsea put the phone on speaker and leaned forward so they could all hear the conversation.

"Can you record on this phone?" Maria asked Zac.

"Yes," Zac nodded. "Chelsea knows how."

Chelsea nodded and carefully found the app to record the conversation.

"You know why, Cat." Marshall's voice rang through the receiver. Cat had him on speaker.

"I won't sign the lyrics of my song you stole over to you. I've found

evidence that it is in fact my song and that you stole it," Cat seethed. "How do you think the great Marshall Myers fans are going to feel then?"

"You won't do that," Marshall called her bluff. "You'd have already done it."

"I'm waiting for my PR manager, lawyer, and manager to get the strategy together to repair the damage to my reputation that your lies caused," Cat told him.

"Let them try," Marshal said smugly. "At the end of the day, my fans are not going to believe you over me."

"Oh, yes, I think they will," Cat told him.

"Oh, please, I'm Marshall Myers. My stupid fans adore me and think I'm not capable of stealing anyone's songs." Marshall laughed. "Cat, I bested you before by telling the world your new hit cover song was mine. That was the best lie I've ever told. It shot my failing greatest hits album to number two."

"I didn't see my song on there," Cat said.

"My lawyers advised me not to use it until we had all the details of ownership completely ironed out," Marshall said. "I'm willing to give you your song."

"The song you stole!" Cat corrected.

"Fine, the song I stole from you back and spin some story about me using that to get you back in my life," Marshall laughed. "You see, my fans still think I'm heartbroken over you, they'll believe any lie I spin them right now."

"Now hear me out," Marshall bargained with Cat. "If you write me

three new songs, I'll give you the precious song you and your mother wrote back to you."

"Are you also willing to tell the world it was you, who cheated on me on numerous occasions, that ended my marriage?" Cat asked him. "As well as retracting your lies about trying to take your own life because of me. While you're at it you can also tell them you were never in a coma but living it up with my money in the Bahamas with your latest floozy?"

"Now why would I tell them that?" Marshall laughed. "That holiday was not as much fun as I thought it would be. I had to keep hidden most of the time so no one would recognize me and realize I wasn't ever in a coma, nor had I attempted suicide."

"Your lies will catch up with you, Marshall," Cat warned him.

"Not me," Marshall bragged. "I have a gift for spinning a story."

"A pity that gift doesn't extend to writing your own songs," Cat said. "Just how many of your other girlfriends' or wives' songs have you stolen?"

"Oh, I see you've been talking to someone?" Marshall said. "We both know I can't write music to save my life. I've always had to rely on ghostwriters or other more talented musicians writing for me." There was a pause. "But I'm not going to admit that to any audience."

"You really don't even care how many of your past partners you've ruined by stealing their songs, do you?" Cat said, disgust lacing her voice.

"There's a sucker born every second." Marshall laughed again. "It's not my fault most of the women I've gone out with are not too bright."

"That is an appalling thing to say," Cat hissed. "Why are we stopping at the car rental place?"

"We need to switch cars, my bodyguards will keep driving this car so if your useless bodyguard back there does wake up before we've left, he'll follow the wrong car," Marshall explained. "Now come on, and remember we have your housekeeper, Debbie."

"It's Daphne, you idiot!" Daphne's voice bellowed through the receiver.

"Don't worry, they won't harm her unless you don't cooperate," Marshall warned her.

"I know you're a thief and a liar, Marshall but when did you become a thug?" Cat asked him.

"This is my career, Cat," Marshall said. "I'm not going to let anyone or anything get in the way of the new career high I'm on."

There was background noise, and the sound of a car door opening.

"Daphne, hang in there, help will be on its way soon," Cat said softly.

"I'm fine, child, but I can't let you go with that oaf!" Daphne said.

"It's okay Daphne," Cat assured her. "Please just do as they say. I don't want anything happening to you. Trust me, I'll be okay."

"Enough chit-chat," Marshall's voice dripped with impatience. "We need to get to Billings. My private jet is fueled and ready to go."
"You have a private jet now?" Cat said.

"It belongs to Danna Ray," Marshall told her. "I'm dating her now."

"Oh, you mean you're bleeding her dry now?" Cat corrected.

"Here's the car," Marshall ignored Cat's statement.

"A red Mustang?" Cat said. "Really! I thought you wanted to be as incon-spicuous as possible?"

"This is me blending in," Marshall told her. "Now get in the car."

"Okay!" Cat hissed back. "I didn't even know Brady's Car Rental hired Mustangs."

"It was pre-ordered especially for me," Marshall bragged. "I'm a big name now so people basically do my bidding."

"How nice for you," Cat said sarcastically.

"Which is the fastest route to Billings?" Marshall asked her.

Cat gave him the route and an estimated time it would take to get there before giving him directions.

"I'll call Wallace and let them know which way they are head-ed." West looked at Maria. "May I borrow your phone? I left mine at Big Valley Ranch."

"Sure." 'Maria handed West her phone.

Chelsea sat back and kept listening to Cat's conversation with Marshall.

They were nearly in Lewistown when Zac spotted David's pickup truck on the side of the road. He pulled up behind it. Zac and West jumped out of the car, running to find David. He was lying in a ditch next to his vehicle. West bent down and felt for a pulse.

"He's okay," West told Zac. "He has a huge lump on the back of his head though."

"David!" Zac patted David's face. "Wake up, buddy."

David's eyes flitted open and he looked confused until he focused on Zac.

"Cat and Daphne!" David sat up too fast and winced then pinched the bridge of his nose. "That idiot Marshall Myers and his two goons ran us off the road. The one hit me over the head with something. The last thing I saw was them dragging Cat and Daphne away."

"It's okay," Zac assured him. "Cat managed to call us, and we know where they are. We've called Wallace and we're heading there now."

"Leave your vehicle," West told David. "We'll get you a tow. It looks like the whole side of it is bashed in."

"Great!" David said, holding his head as Zac pulled him up.

West and Zac helped David get the stuff from his pickup and lock it.

"I'm West, by the way," West introduced himself to David.

"Oh, you're Cat's manager," David shook West's hand while they walked to Zac's pickup.

David climbed into the back of the car, making Chelsea have to sit in the middle.

"Do you want to swap places?" Maria asked Chelsea. "Cat told me you hated sitting in the middle."

"I'll be fine," Chelsea smiled gratefully at Maria. "Thank you."

Zac pulled off once everyone was buckled up.

"Is that Cat's voice?" David looked at Chelsea in surprise.

"Yes," Chelsea confirmed. "She managed to call us and has been feeding us information."

"Clever." David smiled.

Chelsea hid her own smile upon seeing the pride and affection sparkling in David's eyes. Chelsea was right. Something was definitely brewing between Cat and David.

THE CALM BEFORE THE STORM

Epilogue

_C_at was getting worried as she knew her phone's battery was quite low. She knew that Zac had picked up his phone, but Cat couldn't even check her phone to see if they were still connected. She knew Marshall wouldn't really hurt her or least Cat didn't think he would. He needed her but she was still uncertain what his bodyguards would do to Daphne. That was the wild card here or Cat would've stopped this stupidity of Marshall's right away. She swallowed down her rising anger and thought about what this would mean for her if Marshall was caught. Cat didn't wish anyone, even Marshall, ill will but from where she was sitting right now, the creep deserved it.

"What the heck?" Marshall said.

Cat looked up and saw a roadblock ahead of them, "Oh, there's been a lot of trouble in this area lately with cattle and horse theft," she lied. "They've been setting up these roadblocks randomly every day for the past month."

"Just my luck!" Marshall hit the steering wheel impatiently. "Remember to just keep cool, we're on our way to Billings together and of your own free will. I still have Dory."

"Daphne, her name is Daphne," Cat corrected him again and couldn't keep the impatience from her voice. "You have my word."

Marshall pulled up to the roadblock and an officer approached the car. He slid his window down and put on his famous Marshall Myers charm. Whipping off his sunglasses so the police officer would realize who he was.

"Good day officer," Marshall greeted the man with a big smile. "What seems to be the problem?"

"Would you mind showing me your license and registration please?" The office leaned down to the window.

"Sure," Marshall reached into his jacket pocket saying. "I'm just getting my wallet."

The officer nodded.

Marshall pulled out his wallet and handed the officer his license. "Here you are, but I'm sure you don't need it to recognize who I am."

"I'm sorry, sir, but we have to check everyone's licenses," the office didn't seem impressed with Marshall's celebrity status. "Would you mind stepping out of the vehicle please, sir?"

"Why?" Marshalls' brows furrowed. "Has my license expired or something?" He joked.

"Please step out of the vehicle, sir," the officer said once again, this time his hand went threateningly to his holster.

"Okay, okay." Marshal held up his hands and got out of the car.

"Are you Marshall Myers?" The police officer asked him

"Do I really have to confirm that?" Marshall looked at the man amazed.

"Please, can you confirm your identity for me, sir?" The police officer said again.

"Yes, I'm the famous country singer, Marshall Myers!" He said pompously. "Would you like my autograph?"

"I would like you to turn around and put your hands on the hood of the car, please," the officer shocked Marshall by saying.

"Are you joking?" Marshall spat. "I'm Marshall freakin' Myers. You can't treat me like this."

"I'm giving you one last chance to cooperate, sir," the officer warned him.

"You're going to hear from my lawyers about this," Marshall grumbled as he spread his hands on the hood of the car. He glanced through the windscreen at Cat and his face turned red with anger. "Are you filming this?"

Cat nodded and gave him a smug smile.

The office patted Marshall down, then took out his handcuffs, pulled Marshall's arms behind, and cuffed him.

"Marshall Myers, you are under arrest for the kidnapping of Cat Sparrow and Daphne Parsons," the office listed off Marshall's offenses and then read him his rights before turning to Cat. "Are you okay, Ms. Sparrow?"

"Thank you, Officer, I'm fine now, a little shaken by this," Cat told him. "Especially as I had to take a restraining order out against Marshall Myers for harassing me."

"Oh, right," the police officer turned back to Marshall. "You also broke the terms of that restraining order."

"I'll get you for this, Cat," Marshall seethed as the officer took him towards the police car. "I'm going to spin such a story this time that you'll have no fans left by the time I'm finished."

"Cat!" Wallace's voice got Cat's attention.

Cat had been so absorbed in getting Marshall on video that she hadn't heard another vehicle stopping behind her. She was surprised to see just how many vehicles had stopped behind them and that she was not the only one recording the incident.

"Wallace," Cat ran to him.

"Are you okay?" Wallace grabbed her by the upper arms and gave her a once-over, looking for any injuries.

"I'm fine," Cat assured him. "Did you find Daphne?"

"Yes, your brother and manager, West, found her." Janine had come with Wallace. "I'm so glad you're okay. You had me worried sick." She hugged Cat.

"Is David okay?" Cat's eyes widened with worry. "I saw him crumple to the ground."

"He's fine," Wallace told Cat. "I can assure you he's taken harder knocks on his thick head."

"How would you know?" Janine looked at Wallace.

"He's my younger brother," Wallace told Janine, shocking Cat.

"You never tell anyone that!" Cat's eyes narrowed as she stared at Wallace.

Her eyes widened again while both of them looked awkwardly and Janine's cheeks flamed.

"Ohhh!" Cat said and grinned, pointing from one to the other. "You two are dating."

"I…" Wallace, filled with his hat and Janine started to inspect her shoes. "Yes, okay!"

"I knew it," Cat said, elated, and hugged them both. "I'm so happy for the both of you."

"Why are you happy for them?" David's voice had her spinning around.

"David!" Without thinking, Cat flew into his arms which closed around her, and pulled her to him. "I was so worried about you."

"If I knew I was going to get this kind of reaction I would've had someone knock me over the head a long time ago," David said for her ears only.

"Funny," Cat said, smiling happily back up at him.

"Ohhh." Janine turned the tables on Cat. "We see now."

"Touché," Cat said, stepping out of David's arms and turning to Janine.

Before she could say anything else she was bombarded by Chelsea, Maria, West, and Zac all taking turns to hug her.

"I'm so glad you're okay, young lady," Daphne said from behind the wall of people surrounding Cat.

"Oh, Daphne." Cat pushed past them to engulf Daphne in a big hug.

"I think we need to get out of here," West advised them. "Cat, I think the world knows where you are now." He pointed to the attention they'd drawn.

"I don't mind," Cat said. "Those nice people just filmed the whole 'Marshall getting arrested' scene."

THE FOLLOWING SATURDAY

All the families from the surrounding ranches attended the barbecue. There were even some of their good friends from other neighboring ranches and Lewistown. Cat had just flown back to town early that morning after appearing on a talk show where the world finally learned the truth about Marshall Myers. The best thing about it was that there was no way Marshall's PR firm, lawyers, or manager could get him out of the mess he was in.

Cat Sparrow was back at the top. Chelsea sighed as she switched off the television.

"Cat, I'm so happy for you," Chelsea told her. "So, what are your plans?"

"I'm going to tell you three something I have not told anyone yet," Cat looked at Chelsea, Maria, and Ashley who were all standing in the living room with her. "I'm retiring from Country singing, or at least taking a long break. I want to concentrate on saving all of our land and getting to the bottom of the problems we're having."

"Really?" Ashley, Maria, and Chelsea all said at once.

"Really." Cat smiled. "Besides, I'm seriously thinking of going on that date David asked me to go on."

Chelsea was so happy, she clapped and jumped with glee like a teenage girl. But she wasn't the only one, Maria and Ashley both joined in Chelsea's joy.

"Zac and I are also going on our first official date," Chelsea told them.

"So, you had the talk with him, then?" Cat grinned.

"That day you and Daphne were kidnapped, we kissed," Chelsea admitted and felt her cheeks heat up. "Then the next day he came over to Mountain Rise and he had the chat with me."

"I'm so happy for you," Ashley hugged her.

"Wow, Chels, that is such good news," Maria also hugged Chelsea.

"Well, that's two of you going down the relationship path," Ashley said with a sparkle in her eyes. "That leaves only one other person in this room we need to find happiness for."

All eyes turned to Maria.

"Ooh, no!" Maria gave them a horrified sideways glance and held up both hands defensively. "No, no!" She shook her head emphatically. "No way."

"It'll happen when it happens," Chelsea assured Maria.

"Who knows, it might already be happening!" Ashley grinned slyly over the rim of the wine glass she was taking a sip of.

"What's going on here?" Maria's eyes narrowed suspiciously.

"Nothing," Cat said innocently.

"Don't you think it's been lovely and quiet around here lately?" Maria changed the subject.

"What do you mean?" Cat asked her.

"There has been no trouble on the land for a few days now," Maria pointed out.

"I know, it's been so marvelous." Ashley breathed a sigh of relief. "Especially after whoever was doing this started to expand the trouble to all the ranches on this side of Lewistown."

"That doesn't mean they've stopped," Cat pointed out. "They've probably just retreated until the heat from the last incident cools off, and this Marshall fiasco dies down."

"Well, whatever it is," Chelsea said. "I'm glad the trouble seems to have gone for now."

"We'd better get the rest of the snacks outside before we have anarchy," Maria said. "I also need a refill." She held up her glass.

Maria was the first to leave the living room to walk towards the kitchen. Chelsea, Cat, and Ashley followed her. In the kitchen they each of them picked up a plate of food and walked out the back door. They were just putting them on the table when a loud crack echoed through the air. The world seemed to go into slow motion around Chelsea.

"What in the blazes?" Maria hissed as she started to run. "Brett!" She shouted.

Chelsea's head turned to follow where Maria was running to and her eyes widened in shock as she saw Brett, Maria's brother, lying on the ground bleeding. Wallace was running towards where Brett was lying. Zac and David were crouched down next to Brett. While West turned and ran towards the house where they were standing with Ryan Beckett and Billy, Ashley's next to him. As they ran, they grabbed a slow child or helped someone up who'd fallen.

The rest of the people piled into the kitchen while Ryan and Billy stopped to usher Chelsea, Cat, and Ashley into the house. Chelsea tried to fight them off wanting to run after Maria so she could help Brett. But after Ryan handed the child, he held to Billy he all but picked Chelsea up and put her into the house. As Ryan turned to go back out Chelsea saw West grab Maria who fought against him to get Brett, but West held onto her. She saw Zac and David manage to lift Brett. As they did shot rang out, forcing Zac and David to crouch as low as they could while Wallace sheltered them with his body they headed to the house.

"Do you have a rifle?" Ryan asked Chelsea who nodded and ran to the gun safe.

She unlocked it, and before she knew it all five of the rifles and some of the ammunition was taken by some of the other men who were at the barbeque.

"We need to cover Wallace, David, and Zac so they can bring Brett inside," Ryan turned to Liam. "Are you going to be able to help him?"

"Yes," Liam said, turning to Chelsea. "Do you still have all the medical equipment you had for your mother?"

"I do," Chelsea confirmed. Thank goodness she hadn't gotten around to taking it all back. "I'll help Liam."

"Thank you," Liam said.

"I'm phoning emergency services," Cat told them.

The men managed to provide cover fire while Zac, David, and Wallace brought Brett inside. It wasn't long after that that the rescue services and police arrived. But by the time the commotion of their arrival settled down it was to find that the shots had been a diversion.

While everyone had to retreat inside the shooters had managed to rustle up some of the horses and most of what was left of Mountain Rises cattle was gone. "Oh, no!" Chelsea breathed, her eyes misting with tears.

"We're going to get your livestock back." Ryan Beckett stepped up behind Chelsea and gave her shoulder a reassuring squeeze. "We are also going to find who is behind this."

"It's time for all of us to forget our petty feuds or problems with each other," Zac stepped up to say, getting everyone's attention. "Today, we were like sitting ducks and were lulled into a false sense of security because there's been no trouble in days."

"You had to go and say it, didn't you, Maria?" Cat whispered.

"Sorry." Maria's brow furrowed.

"You should've just answered their questions about your relationship status," Cat pointed out, trying to lighten the mood.

"Brett's going to be fine," Chelsea came up to them. "Liam managed to stop the bleeding and the bullet was through and through."

"Oh, thank goodness. Can I see him?" Maria asked.

"Of course," Chelsea said.

Maria went to see Brett while Zac continued his speech and laid down plans to save the ailing ranches while also investigating who was behind these attacks. When he was finished, the room erupted into applause and Chelsea's heart warmed. Uncle Callum had always said nothing brings people together like death, marriage, and war. They were fighting away against an invisible enemy cowardly hiding in the shadows. They were attacking when they knew the people they were ganging up against were at their most vulnerable.

Chelsea's stomach burned with anger. They had taken her livestock and some of hers as well as her neighbors' prize horses. She knew that she was no longer going to hide away in the shadows afraid of the enemy. Chelsea looked up and her eyes locked with Zac's. Her heart filled with so much love and pride she thought she was going to burst.

Zac inclined his head indicating for her to follow him. Her heart did a few summersaults as she made her way through the sea of people into the study. Zac closed and locked the door before pulling her into his arms and crushing his lips to hers.

Chelsea's arms immediately went around his neck as she lost herself in the kiss. When he pulled away, he dropped down onto one knee.

"I know I don't have a ring on me," Zac told her. "But Chelsea, I've never stopped loving you and I never will. I know we're supposed to go on our first date but if today's proved anything it's that we don't know what tomorrow is going to bring." He took her hand. "I love you, and I would love you to be my wife again."

"Oh, Zac." Chelsea swallowed the emotion that was bubbling up inside of her. "I love you so much too. I'm so sorry for walking out on you fourteen years ago. But I never stopped loving you either. It's always been only you in my heart."

Chelsea reached down and cupped Zac's handsome face. "Yes, I'll marry you again."

Zac stood up and pulled her to him for another head-spinning kiss.

"But we're going to have to get married soon," Zac warned her. "Because I'm back in here today. There is no way I'm leaving you on your own."

"What about Cupids Bow?" Chelsea asked him.

"Wallace is going to be there," Zac told her, "while David and West will be at Big Valley."

"And of course, no one can protect his land or family at Four Lakes better than Ryan," Chelsea said.

"Exactly," Zac agreed. "We are going to be setting up radios, and equipment, on each of the farms on this side of Lewistown."

"In other words, you're amassing an army of ranches?" Chelsea smiled.

"We have to," Zac nodded. "Someone is trying to drive us off the land we've had for generations. We're not going to take that lying down."

"No, we are not!" Chelsea sighed and let Zac pull her in for a hug.

"No one comes after our families like they've been doing," Zac's voice was filled with conviction. This had to end now!

THE SERIES CONTINUES

ARE YOU READY TO READ Big Valley Ranch, book 3 of the Montana Country Inn Romance Series?

To read the next book in this series, go to www.amazon.com/dp/B09WY35G65

ALSO BY AMY RAFFERTY

To dive into your next read, go to https://www.amyraffertyauthor.com/

STAY UPDATED WITH ME

Thank you so much for purchasing or downloading my book! I am grateful to all my amazing readers.

To stay updated on all my latest books, newsletters, freebies and beautiful photos from the fabulous locations I write about, why not join my VIP group?

I will send you regular pictures of La Jolla Cove, San Diego and the Florida Gulf Beaches where I try to spend as much time as I can. I live in San Diego, my own 'Garden Of Eden' and I am in love with the sea and the beaches in the area. They inspire me to write lots of beachy mystery romance fiction to share with my awesome readers like you. To join me go to https://landing.mailer lite.com/webforms/landing/y6w2d2

You will be asked for your email. You also get a FREE BOOK whenever you sign-up!

FREE BOOK

To get your FREE copy of Cody Bay Inn Prequel - Nantucket Calling go to www.amazon.com/B0992NFTY1

ABOUT THE AUTHOR

Amazon #1 Best-Seller, Amy Rafferty is a contemporary romance author of feel-good beach romance reads with heartwarming stories embracing humor and love.

Born in New York, previously a Lawyer, she now lives in San Diego with her beautiful children and cats!

Aside from writing, publishing and running her home, she spends as much time as she can visiting the beautiful San Diego and Florida beaches where she has family and friends. She calls San Diego her 'Garden of Eden', inspiring her to write clean and wholesome romance novels incorporating mystery, suspense and adventures for her characters as they find a way to open their hearts and let true love in.

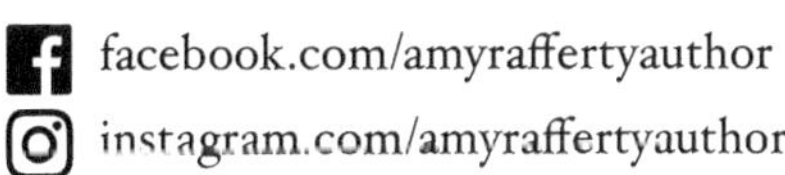

facebook.com/amyraffertyauthor

instagram.com/amyraffertyauthor